THE COMPANY OF GHOSTS

THE COMPANY OF GHOSTS

followed by
SOME USEFUL ADVICE FOR
APPRENTICE PROCESS-SERVERS

by
LYDIE SALVAYRE

Translation and Preface by
CHRISTOPHER WOODALL

DALKEY ARCHIVE PRESS
NORMAL · LONDON

Originally published in French as *La Compagnie des spectres* by Éditions du Seuil (1997) and *Quelques conseils utiles aux élèves huissiers* by Éditions Verticales (1997)

La Compagnie des spectres copyright © 1997 by Éditions du Seuil
Quelques conseils utiles aux élèves huissiers copyright © 1997 by Éditions du Seuil / Éditions Verticales
Translation copyright © 2006 by Christopher Woodall
Preface copyright © 2006 by Christopher Woodall

First edition, 2006

Library of Congress Cataloging-in-Publication Data

Salvayre, Lydie.
   [Compagnie des spectres. English]
   The company of ghosts / Lydie Salvayre ; translated by Christopher Woodall.— 1st ed.
      p. cm.
   ISBN 1-56478-350-2 (pbk. : alk. paper)
   I. Woodall, Christopher, translator. II. Title.

PQ2679.A52435C6613 2006
843'.914—dc22
                                                    2005049209

*Ouvrage publié avec le concours du
Ministère français chargé de la Culture – Centre National du Livre.*
[This Work has been published thanks to the
French Ministry of Culture – National Book Center.]

Partially funded by a grant from the Illinois Arts Council, a state agency.

Dalkey Archive Press is a nonprofit organization located at
Milner Library (Illinois State University) and distributed in the UK
by Turnaround Publisher Services Ltd. (London).

www.dalkeyarchive.com

Printed on permanent/durable acid-free paper and bound in the
United States of America.

As a form of creative writing, literary translation entails a quite peculiar amalgam of freedom and constraint. Liberated from the chore of creating a plot and of deciding what (if anything) will happen on the next page, translators readily submit to decisions that have already been made for them: if a particular character in the writer's text goes out at 10:00, say, the translator cannot (without some exceptionally good reason) have him going out at 9:55.

Having entered into this division of labor, the translator is blissfully free to concentrate on word choice, idiom, syntax, the sound and rhythm of the new text—in a word, its style. For it is the patient transposition and mimicking of style that are the translator's forte, and the source of much of the pleasure that the process of translation affords. First and foremost, translators are stylistic chameleons: while all but the most protean of writers compose their oeuvre in a single or narrowly limited set of individual styles, the very essence of literary translation is the willingness to write in a new—indeed a *foreign*—way, and an openness to experimentation.

Yet the seemingly infinite choices that confront translators as they work their way through a novel, story, or poem are again constrained, indeed persistently *tested*, by constant reference back to the author's text. The translator proceeds Janus-headed, glancing forward to the new text as it takes shape on paper, but also back over his shoulder to the old text, sanctified as it is by prior publication and now further dignified by the very fact of its translation and promise of new life in a new language.

When lucky enough to choose what we translate, translators may sometimes be torn between, on the one hand, playing it safe by accepting a piece of work similar to something "tackled" in the past, and, on the other, taking a risk, embracing a text whose shape and sound in our own language we may, at the outset, barely be able to imagine.

In the case of Lydie Salvayre's *La Compagnie des spectres*, I wanted to translate this novel almost from the moment I laid my hands on it. On the strength of a review that I had read in *Le Monde*, I rushed out to buy it and then fell in love with a text that I read in delectable doses over several weeks. It wasn't long before I found myself wondering how Salvayre's overlapping narrators, extreme registers, and heavy irony might be voiced in English, and I was soon trying out random passages to see.

What excites me most in *La Compagnie des spectres* and what I have therefore sought hardest to preserve in *The Company of Ghosts* is the novel's stylistic quirkiness and its insistent juxtaposition of unbridled excess and claustrophobic restraint: the process-server is punctiliously impassive to the point of inhumanity; the teenage Louisiane lurches between a bottled-up formality, studded with incongruous classical erudition, and the babbling confession of her uncommon pitch of sexual wretchedness; Rose—Louisiane's deranged, reclusive mother—shuttles, now prophetic, now uncomprehending, between the horrors of her childhood experiences in Vichy France and her mordant commentary on present-day French society; while Rose's own mother, politically naive and instinctively anarchistic, is depicted in the throes of a passionate and doomed revolt against the icy autocracy of Marshal Pétain's État Français.

The cross-contamination between these stories and the way that the narrators' voices not only skip between historical epochs but also at times seep into one another—often with barely a comma by way of signposting—lends this writing its subversive edge, uncovering the present in the past and implicating the past in the present, exposing continuities of authoritarianism in behavior and language just as casually and naturally as Rose Mélie mistakes the intruding process-server for a Fascist thug straight out of the 1940s.

I should like to express my gratitude to Annick Gros and Christophe Bulka who listened patiently and responded thoughtfully to my many queries about specific words, phrases, and passages in *La Compagnie des spectres* and *Quelques conseils*.

Christopher Woodall

2006

THE COMPANY OF GHOSTS

For Marie,
for Montsé

But you will say: what is the point of stirring up all this trash of which the universe has grown so heartily sick? . . . Fine, I tell you, be good, calm down, for the transition from madness to a life of reason can be effected only by drawing up an inventory of the dark deliberations that unleashed the dark urges which, in their turn, breaking the bonds of every custom and fleeing into the day and the century, thought themselves able to adorn with the plumage of others and the pomp of their own lies the very light of life, yet all was twilight and ruin.

—Carlo Emilio Gadda, *Eros and Priapus*,
Translated from Italian by Christopher Woodall

And so there I was, gushing politely at the process-server, Yes Mr Process-Server, No Mr Process-Server, calculating that however unnatural it felt this was the way to make a good impression and maybe persuade him to cancel or at least to moderate his orders, when I saw the bedroom door fly open and my mother appear in her dirty nightdress, girdled at the waist by that hideous fanny pack that she never let out of her sight, just in case, she said, she were to be led *manu militari* to an internment camp and, as I was saying, I saw her appear there and scream at the process-server, Is it Darnand who's sent you?

I immediately led her back into what we laughingly referred to as her "apartments," while requesting the process-server, who had lost none of his composure, even if, I presume, he must have felt rather disconcerted, to be so kind as to wait a few moments.

And then, having taken my mother back to her bedroom, in order to hide her and, if I may put it this way, to neutralize the danger she represented, returning to the hall where I'd confined him, he read out:

On this day, April 15, 1997, the undersigned, Maître Echinard, Process-Server-at-Law, officially appointed to the aforesaid position by the civil authorities of the town of Créteil, and residing at no. 44 rue Violette, herewith delivers to Mademoiselle Rose Mélie, residing at no. 10 cité des Acacias, apartment number 230, floor 12, Créteil, the undersigned being present and speaking, as is stated hereinafter in the report of notification, on behalf of Monsieur Marcel Leducq, of French nationality, born on August 10, 1930, in Paris (twelfth arrondissement), in retirement, residing in Paris (eleventh arrondissement) at 16 rue Camille Desmoulins, electing residence at the offices of the undersigned, acting on the basis of a final ruling handed down on June 2, 1996, following due hearing of both parties, by the Juge d'Instance of the town of Créteil, in view of your non-execution of the injunction placed upon you to declare the name and address of your employer or the details of your bank accounts in order for your incomings to be distrained, a formal summons to . . .

TWO

And while the process-server mumbled his way through this seizure summons, which to me was utterly, but utterly, incomprehensible, I tried to figure out what remote chances I might possess of saving from this damned inventory the few items that I loved and, in particular, the TV set, without which, I thought, it would be impossible for me to live.

Oh, do please come in, I insisted the moment the process-server had terminated his gibberish, and I ceremoniously opened the door to the living room. I hoped that such thoroughly Japanese manners might conceal the indescribable mess that reigned in our apartment. Excuse this disorder, I said, though I very nearly said "dump." The process-server maintained a perfectly expressionless face as he swept the room with a gloomy eye. Are you in possession of a motorized land vehicle? he asked me point-blank. It was a curious gambit. What? I said. Do you have an auto? he then asked with a dash of impatience. No, I said.

The process-server at once launched into the inventory and inscribed in a black notebook that he took from his briefcase: one macaronic-style wall thermometer depicting a frightened doe behind foliage carved in copper, which seems to us of no value; a fan possessing a wooden handle and black fabric decorated with red roses and bearing the legend RECUERDOS DE GRANADA, which we deem of little worth; an oval frame, made of gilded wood, containing a photo . . .

And at the precise instant when the process-server, planted in front of the photograph of Uncle Jean, was punctiliously noting down these various particulars, my mother burst in again, in her dirty nightdress, girdled by the hideous fanny pack that never left her and that contained her jewels, some small change, the portrait of Uncle Jean and the one of me, and, with her crazed face, crazed look and crazed voice, screamed at the process-server, Is it Darnand who's sent you?

A silence ensued. A dismayed silence, it goes without saying. A perilous silence.

Pardon me? asked the process-server.

I felt as overwhelmed with shame as would any girl my age. Assuming a perfectly hypocritical air of pained kindness, I whispered to my mother, Mama, you are tired, you ought to have a little nap, hoping this would compel her to leave immediately. But I was deluding myself as to the power of my words, for no sooner were they uttered than they sank without a trace, and my mother didn't move.

I then turned to the process-server who, since his "Pardon me," had been standing still and mute, observing my mother with the same cold look as though she were a footstool or a cheese dish. Please be so good (so good!) as to bear with me one second, I murmured to him. Then I grabbed my mother by the arm and, driving my nails into her flesh to demonstrate my determination, I dragged her off to her bedroom, which she ought never to have left, and, in an abrupt tone that I thought might have a narcotic or at least an inhibiting effect upon her, I urged her to go to bed and behave herself. This, I told her, as I leaned close to her ear, is no time to play games. It was then that I noticed that she smelled bad.

Have I told you, my dear, my mother began as soon as she had lain down on her bed, that it was seven in the evening when (I knew what came next by heart) . . .

. . . when your Uncle Jean opened the door of the Café des Platanes? And then the Jadre twins, whom everyone in the village called J1 and J2, stepped in front of him. Didn't you read the notice? J1 said to him (the notice bore the words NO JEWS NO DOGS). Then J2 kicked the door closed again, and your Uncle Jean, who hadn't realized the danger he was in, without reflecting on what he was doing, slid his foot into the gap. And turning it over and over in my mind, my mother said, I have come to the view, my dear, that it was because, being the young man that he was, he slid his foot into the opening of a door that your uncle was condemned. It was that minuscule act of resistance that impelled the Jadre twins to commit their barbarous act. Because in those days the Jadre twins did not allow anyone to resist them, any hint of resistance and they would crush it beneath their boots. Ever since they had paraded through the streets of Toulouse under the eyes of Cheneaux de Leyritz, General Schubert in person, Bézagu and all the other eminences, the Jadre twins thought themselves the masters of the village and, since they thought themselves the masters, others took them to be so.

Mama, please, stop it, I said to her, thinking of the process-server I had abandoned in the living room.

And then, my mother continued as though she hadn't heard me, as though my words were completely unrelated to the thing that so wholly possessed her, J1 and J2 backed your uncle out onto the pavement, punching him in the chest and knocking the wind out of him, after which they backed him over to the waste ground that bordered the train station, you know, where the parking lot is now. Because that day, my dear, the Jadre twins wanted something to happen, but they didn't yet know what. They wanted something dreadful and definitive to happen that would consecrate them in the eyes of Darnand's Militia. For months they had been waiting for the moment when they would be able to distinguish themselves and at last gain admittance to the Franc-Garde, Darnand's elite militia. For their secret dream was to join the Franc-Garde and to march down the Champs Elysées in parade-dress wearing the skull-and-crossbones insignia that you may have seen placed on the walls of the headquarters. But to earn this advancement, they had to show they were worthy, and in order to accomplish this the Jadre brothers were ready to do whatever was necessary.

And then my mother said, in a voice that was beginning to crack, My brother looked them in the eyes with that look of his that had the gentleness of a girl, he looked them in the eyes hoping that by the sole strength of his look he might yet halt the terrible sequence of actions that he felt was about to begin. But the opposite happened. The Jadre twins had only one idea, to beat this look that was gentle and straight as a lance, till it broke. Remember, my dear, that it is dangerous to look wicked people in the eyes, because then they are afraid that you will discover there the appalling secrets of their souls that all pity has deserted: the fear of being read and deciphered renders the wicked to their wickedness. Do not forget this.

Mama, please, calm down, I repeated, and the idea suddenly came to me of stuffing a rag in her mouth.

And then, Mama said, getting enraged, J1 kicked your uncle in the stomach twice as hard as before, blows that made an odd sound, and your uncle fell backward, but he didn't yet have any premonition of his death, You're mad, he told them, catching his breath, Don't be idiots, he said. And while he tried to get to his feet, J2 suggested to J1, In the balls, kick him in the balls, and then J1 aimed his boot between your uncle's legs, making him scream with pain. He's scared, said J1. He's shitting in his pants, said J2. He's flunked his lesson, said J1, and the twins began to laugh. Because you have to know, my dear, that the Jadre twins could barely write their own names in capital letters and perhaps envied my brother who had been so brilliant at school, perhaps my brother died because he had been better than they at French and Geography, perhaps it's that stupid, Mama said in despair.

That's bullshit, I said, in an effort to interrupt my mother, for I could imagine the process-server pacing up and down the living room, exasperated, his eyes fixed on his watch, and in a terrible mood.

Your uncle stood paralyzed like an animal awaiting its death, Mama continued in a pitiful voice. Aren't you going to call for your Mummy? J1 asked him. Or don't you want to bother her while she's fucking? Who is it, which buddy of Gaga-gaulle is screwing your Mummy now? Don't you know the name of the Kike that's screwing her? Are you going to answer, you son of a bitch? But the more I think about it, Mama said, the more persuaded I am that the Jadre twins didn't hit your uncle in order to wring confessions from him, as one is often tempted to believe, on the contrary they hit him in order to annihilate within him the very possibility of speaking, they hit him to make him completely silent, since

14

for the Jadre twins the speech of your uncle threatened to reveal at any moment something completely unheard of and certainly far beyond their control, at least beyond the reach of their weapons. Nobody is powerful, Mama went on, unless they can prevent others from speaking, with whatever means that takes. Power consists in closing the mouths of others, Mama said, but as for me nobody will make me be quiet, she declared raising her voice, neither Putain nor Darnand, nor anybody, she yelled.*

Mama, you are now going to shut up, OK? I said to her. I couldn't help it. She was really beginning to get on my nerves with her whining. This whole thing is ancient history, it's time to change the record, I shouted at her, with all the anger that had accumulated in me over the last five minutes—what am I saying? I mean over days, over months, in fact throughout the whole eighteen interminable years of my life so far.

My brother got up very gently and backed toward the tracks, my mother said in a voice that choked back her crying. Then J1 pushed him, with all the force of his hatred, and your uncle fell backward onto the embankment. Then the twins kicked him till he slid down onto the tracks, and your uncle's head struck the fishplate, and your uncle, my dear, who had never yet thought of death, your eighteen-year-old uncle beseeched heaven that death would come quickly, for he now

---

* *Putain,* Rose Mélie's obsessively repeated term for Marshal Pétain, is a slang term for prostitute, roughly equivalent to "whore" or "hooker." Pétain headed the pro-Nazi French State, based in the small southern French town of Vichy, which governed France from 1940 until 1944. Later on in the novel (see Chapter Nineteen), it becomes clear that Rose sometimes employs the word *Putain* to stand not only for Marshal Pétain, but also for his fellow-collaborators such as Bousquet and Darnand, and indeed for the entire collaborationist project in general.

wanted to die. And I often wonder, my dear, what he thought about when he realized that he was about to die. Some regret? A face he had once caressed? Or already the abyss? And then J1 undid his fly and peed on your uncle's face and said, That's to wake you up, and the Jadre twins began to laugh. These images are going to kill me, my dear, Mama cried, they're going to kill me, she cried.

Mama, be quiet, I told you to be quiet, I said to her, though I knew there was no point repeatedly telling her to be quiet, just as there was no point reminding her that her brother's death was fifty-four years ago, and that it was no longer of any interest to anybody, and that Uncle Jean was nothing more to me than a faded photo hanging on the hallway wall and the name I attach to everything that hurts.

For nothing could stop my mother when she reentered the past and plunged back into her disastrous childhood. For my mother, almost as though she enjoyed it, could spend entire days wailing, and entreating heaven to hear her cries and to console her. For my mother was disturbed, Dr Logos was quite emphatic on this point. Dr Logos, arguing that a normal emotion in humans ought to last no more than five minutes, let's say ten, had stated, scientifically, that Mama was disturbed.

Cracking the hammer of his pistol, J2 knelt down close to the face of your uncle, then rested the mouth of the barrel against his temple and slowly, lovingly, made him turn his head, slowly, lovingly, from one side then to the other, from one side then to the other. And he began to sing *On bended knees, we took our oath, Militia men, to perish singing, if need be, for the New France* . . . And while J2 was singing, J1 was crushing the heel of his boot against your uncle's temple. And Uncle Jean fainted.

That's enough, I said to my mother, through clenched teeth, I've had quite enough of these horror stories. What with the TV and you, I've had my fill, I quietly hissed, not wishing to be overheard by the process-server whom I had left stranded in the living room.

And J1 got up, my mother said, went over to the fence that edged the field bordering the tracks and tore off a piece of wire. Then he came back to your uncle, tied his wrists tight to one rail so that the wire dug into his flesh, while J2 tied his ankles to the other rail. They left him right there on the tracks. Like a piece of trash. Meanwhile your grandmother searched for him up and down the village streets, in every direction, with a horrible premonition in her heart. Why didn't I die instead of him? Mama said, and her voice cracked. Always this never-ending wailing, I thought.

It was March 13, 1943.

It was yesterday.

At eight in the evening, Mama said, the Jadre twins return to the café. They drink. Liter after liter. They aren't thirsty, but they drink. They raise their glasses. They drink a toast. To the health of France. They empty their glasses in a single gulp. Then they bang them on the bar. Another one! They say they have Lecussan and Marty on their side, that they're working together, hand in hand, they repeat several times "hand in hand," they're proud of it. They say, We give it all we've got, we're not afraid of anyone, we're not like those cowards who talk and talk but do nothing—another one! As for Commies, we kill them with a pickax, goddamn right, J1 called out, or with something else, J2 says chuckling, we bleed them like pigs, for Christ's sake, J1 says, now we have something to believe in, J2 says, we can raise our heads, J1 says, but the twins are too drunk to raise their heads. The Fatherland must be defended, J2 says as he hoists his glass, the sons of bitches have shat all over it. J1 copies him. They drink a toast. To the health of France. To the trampled Fatherland. Then they empty their glasses. Down in one.

I've had enough, stop, I ordered my mother, without unclenching my lips. She really knows how to exasperate me. My mother looked at me without seeing me, with those crazed eyes she always had when she began talking about her brother.

No one can say how your grandmother endured life after finding your Uncle Jean the following morning bound to the tracks, his eyes staring at something immense and his body in bits like a dog killed on the highway. And you see, my dear, what tortures me, is to think . . .

I didn't want to hear what came next. I knew that if I let her speak she would soon start to scream. I didn't want to hear her scream. I was sick of hearing her scream. I said to her, But you're going to shut it, right, you're going to shut it finally, right? I searched for her medications in all the jumble on top of her bedside table. I measured her drops into a glass. I tripled the dosage, so she'd shut up. Drink! I said to her in the harshest possible tone. It was the only way to make her be quiet. She looked at me in fear. She stammered that her mother . . .

I don't give a damn about your mother, go to sleep.

My mother does nothing but sleep or scream. You can understand why I prefer her to sleep. I tell myself sometimes that the mammoth dosages I give her will knock her out for good. And sometimes I wish she were dead. And sometimes I fear it. But it's only mammoth dosages that control the screaming. As for her madness, that withstands everything. I've finally realized that it is stronger than her medications, stronger than she is herself and stronger than death. I've become convinced that there is no sleeping pill that could knock out her memory, no remedy in the world that could ever control her grief. So much so that I have the feeling that, even dead, her grief, intact, will survive her, besides it's what she often says herself in her delirium, she says I shall die and take to my tomb the image of my dead brother ripped to pieces on the railroad tracks at Venerque and that of Putain whom I saw the same day on the front page of *La Garonne* drinking his hot chocolate and standing alongside his wife, and that of Bousquet announcing his latest tactics to the press, and these images, Mama said in that grandiloquent tone of hers that I so detest, these images will contaminate the Earth forever and blight the life of those who remain. You understand, my dear? I understand, Mama, I told her, to get some peace. You are not really listening, she said, to what I'm trying to explain to you. On March 23, 1943, my dear, the foundation of everything collapsed and Pity died forever, said my mother who, in her madness, thinks she's a soothsayer, a Pythoness. Sometimes that's what I call her: the Pythia of Créteil. What vision does the Pythia of Créteil have for us today? I say to her. That makes her laugh.

Before leaving her bedroom, just to reassure her, I checked that her shutters were closed, then I rummaged through the wardrobe and got down on all fours to take a peek under her bed where yellowed books and twenty-year-old magazines were stacked in the dust, praying to heaven that the process-server didn't catch a glimpse of me in this pose through the open door. There's no one here, I announced, sleep, you have no reason to be afraid, sleep. Mama implored me to check again. With enemies like these, you could never be too careful, she said. I went through the rigmarole a second time.

Then Mama lay down amid the books that cluttered the bedsheets and the scraps of paper on which she was writing her life, and drew her knees up to her belly in order not to disturb our cat Camille who was busy meditating in the Sphinx position. Next to her pillow she placed the folder containing the Bousquet indictment, the Darnand file and her writings on Marshal Pétain, whom she called quite simply Putain, the Whore. I pulled the blanket up, tucked it in, and patted her ink-stained sheet.

Sleep.

Don't leave me alone, she pleaded, looking unhappily at me, and she began to weep.

Don't cry, I said to her spitefully. If there's one thing in this life that I really hate, it's the sight of people crying.

Don't go, she pleaded.

I stood firm. And left her, if I may put it this way, with her sorrow, taking care to shut the door so that in the living room the sound of her screaming would be muffled. Because my mother even screams herself to sleep. And her screaming wakes her up. And me too. Which drives me crazy. It's Jean who was calling me, she moaned, his legs had been ripped off yet he was still moving around without a crutch to lean on. Are you there, Louisiane? Yes, Mama, I'm here, don't be afraid. And she takes hours to realize that she is indeed in Créteil, in her bedroom, next to me, her little daughter. Yes, it's me, Mama, it's Louisiane, your daughter, I say to her, calm down now, while her bedroom, her body and her thoughts slowly reassemble themselves.

I breathed deeply, like at school in the gym doing exercises, breathe in, breathe out, breathe in, breathe out, and I said to myself as I breathed out, She is ruining my life, she is poisoning me, then I returned to the living room where . . .

. . . the process-server was scrupulously jotting down in his little black notebook: six assorted wooden chairs, chipped legs, damaged condition, no particular style, no value . . .

I've kept you waiting, Maître Echinard, I said, please forgive me. I wondered if the moment had come to give him some light refreshment. But I remembered that I had no beverage to offer other than tap water. Besides, the idea occurred to me that I might be trying too hard. The way poor people do. Courtesy okay, I decided, but no obsequiousness.

This was the state of my thinking when I saw my mother (whose conduct rarely now obeyed the dictates of decorum) appear for the third time in the same apparel: a dirty nightdress and that hideous fanny pack hanging from her belt, and yell out, despite the fact that she had just ingested enough neuroleptics to knock out an ox,

Is it Darnand who's sent you?

The process-server said nothing. But I felt horribly embarrassed. Wishing to seem a good daughter, I forced myself to smile, while in my heart of hearts I was furious. I need the patience of an angel, I simpered. After which I charged straight at my mother. She started back in fear. I felt a secret satisfaction. I grabbed her hand and squeezed it hard while applying a slight twist to the knuckles. Let me go or I'll scream, she said trying to break free. I dragged her toward her bedroom without loosening my grip. She came quietly. I always gained the upper hand in the end.

The man whom you mistake for Darnand's lackey, I whispered to her with a sort of cold rage, is none other than Maître Echinard, a process-server by profession, and this process-server, I pronounced slowly, is here to draw up an inventory of our movable assets, with all their contents, with a view to seizure, initially, and eviction, thereafter, eviction, I pronounced slowly: so you see this is not the moment for one of your scenes.

After which I instructed her to put on some if not clean clothes then at least odorless ones, to cease acting like a clown, and to shut her mouth hermetically, her-me-ti-cal-ly, I insisted, because this process-server held our fate in his hands and it was essential, I said softly, that we use great skill with him.

With a levity that confounded me, Mama replied that we had to endure this event philosophically and without departing in the slightest from our normal habits. I find, she said to annoy me further, that you attach excessive importance to this whole "seizure" business. Do not sully your mind with such matters, said Seneca, Mama said: I shall prove to you beyond any doubt that a generous nature is shriveled and debilitated by surrendering to such sordidness. As for me, I have no time for such crap, she said, infuriating me beyond the point of endurance. Upon which, she pirouetted, made her way resolutely to the door, and eyed the process-server from head to foot.

Is it Darnand who's sent you?

It appeared to me that the situation was somewhat compromised. If my mother had set out to confound all my strategies, she could not have gone about it any better. Drop dead, you crazy old bat, I railed inwardly. Her conduct was infuriating me beyond anything I could have imagined possible. But I promised myself I'd get even with her. The moment the process-server left I would attack her head-on, reminding her of all the times I had been packed off into foster care on account of her lapses. Till she whimpered, and begged my forgiveness.

Please Mr Process-Server, I apologized, putting on the afflicted face that circumstances clearly required, do not take umbrage at my mother's words for she's craz . . . for she presents, as you may observe for yourself, some slight mental derangement. My mother, who has suffered a great deal, simultaneously inhabits the past and the present, for grief possesses this strange power, I said, waxing fiendishly metaphysical, that it either destroys time altogether or it throws it completely out of sync, depending. Mama's timeless mind is thus constantly shuttling between the year 1943 and our own, without any regard for official chronology: it's a symptom, it appears, that is particularly intractable to treatment. And this leads her into continual and outlandish blunders. She is forever uncovering similarities between people she sees on television and Putain's gang, as she calls it, a gang of swine who under different guises created all kinds of havoc. She believes that Marshal Pétain is still in government, though it's patently absurd. She mistakes you for one of Darnand's emissaries, God knows why! She asserts that those who are now ruling over us, all these shits, she screams, are enjoining us in a more or less roundabout way to serve family, labor, and Fatherland, have you ever heard such outrageous nonsense? I told you, Mama thinks it's still 1943, the year of her brother's death, which in a sense she commemorates every day, for her brother,

Mr Process-Server, is assassinated every day and every day he is interred, every hour that passes tolls the bell of his death throes, and every one of our evenings is a wake.

For that reason my mother is constantly disoriented, constantly off-center and literally anachronistic. All it takes is a detail for her to be hurled back headlong into 1943, that sinister and unforgettable year, after which she has terrible difficulty returning. All it takes is for her to see a general in uniform on her TV set for her immediately to scream at him and call him Lammerding, La-Merde-Dingue, "The Crazy Shit." Bastard! she starts to scream, Murderer! You sure deserve your name! All it takes is for her to read on the wall of the building across the street the slogan LA FRANCE AUX FRANÇAIS!, FRANCE FOR THE FRENCH!, for her to hurtle through the congested districts of memory, where other people would normally get stuck in a jam, and then land bang in the middle of the annual conference of the fascist Parti des Forces Nouvelles. But this landing, Mr Process-Server, is not always smooth. Sometimes she crashes and it's not a pretty sight: one foot here, the other foot over there, and her soul, between the two, torn to shreds.

When, Mr Process-Server, I attempt to understand my mother, I imagine that she experiences that strange feeling that takes hold of me whenever, traveling by train with my back to the engine, I have the impression that I'm plummeting toward a future that is not ahead of me but behind me, while at the same time the past is throwing itself at me as if to eat me up. Do you follow me? Do my explanations seem clear to you? I don't often come up with the right expression at the right moment. I apologize. I kept on apologizing for things. I would have apologized for existing, if the circumstances had called for it. The way poor people do: they never stop saying they're sorry, it's enough to drive you insane, and they're forever saying thank you.

Put plainly, Monsieur, my mother is mad, I concluded.

If to that you add penury, excruciating boredom, and fear of everything, you will easily understand our situation. The process-server did not look as if he understood. It's complicated, Mr Process-Server, complicated, that's the least one can say. If you discern a way out of the deep sh—forgive me, out of the awful mess we are in, short of international revolution of course, it would be very good of you to apprise me of it. I was talking like a book.

As for this Darnand whom she keeps throwing at you, do you know who he was? I asked the process-server who was now examining the wooden board fixed on the right-hand wall as you come in and decorated with an inscription in gothic letters which said: *If you come to my home, dear friend, you will either arrive too late or depart too soon.* Do you know, Monsieur, who this Darnand was?

FIVE

A monster, Monsieur. A monster who only appeared to be human. A monster whose crimes, Monsieur, filled my childhood with terror. For in my early years I was rocked to sleep to the stories of Darnand and Putain, and I may say that, in short, Darnand and Putain were my wolves, my goblins, and my Bluebeard, just as distressing, just as grotesque and unreal; and the accounts of their depravities, which even as a child I listened to with only one ear, for I sensed already that I had to protect myself from them, deposited in the depths of my memory images of terror that still endure and that rear up at night to pursue me.

But let's return to the odious Darnand, odious according to Mama, I scarcely need point out, Darnand of whose existence most people know nothing. To put it succinctly, Mr Process-Server, Darnand is Mama's personal enemy and, in her eyes, the entelechial figure of evil for, while not possessing their frightening forms, Darnand embodies evil a thousand times better than do horned devils. Mama, I said, has amassed a mass of documents and all sorts of information that she has collected in a somewhat fanciful dossier that she never ceases to add to, subtract from, and embellish. It keeps her occupied.

Mama, who had heard me, went straight into her bedroom, and began to rummage through the papers covering her tiny table, which she pompously called her desk, and succeeded in extracting from the jumble a sheet of cardboard which had been scribbled upon in every direction. Then she came back into the living room, still dressed in her filthy nightdress and her fanny pack and, her head thrown back in the manner of ancient tragedians, her left foot pointing forward at a right angle to her right foot, she declaimed:

Surname Darnand; first name Joseph; nickname Jo or Jojo; occupation torturer; sex male; ancestry one hundred percent French; spouse French; origin Aryan, verified by cephalic index (scale four); height average, 1.67 meters; arches his back to gain a few centimeters; distinctive trait, rectangular moustache the size of a postage stamp stuck above the labial cleft, which one cannot decently refer to as a mouth, sewer would be more appropriate; physiognomy brachycephalic; complexion dark; coat black and dense: a series of characteristics inviting comparison in many ways with the pedigree of the dominated race.

Things were looking bad, very bad, I thought, alarmed, as I listened to my mother. From the standpoint of either taste or morality, her cardboard sheet was nothing less than horrifying and was in danger of repelling the man of law once and for all. I didn't know what to do. Wrongly or rightly, I considered it as dangerous to interrupt her as to endure her horrific ranting. We endured it.

Upon racial examination, Mama read out, the subject presents a stubby penis covered with an abundant and Catholic foreskin, beneath which may be glimpsed two asymmetrical testicles.

Mama, really, I exclaimed, but upon this aposiopesis I remained frozen, a fact which my mother was quick to exploit by continuing to read aloud her vulgar filth.

Primitive and brutal in his manners. Poor school record. Darnand uses few abstract words. Favorite writer: none. Favorite composer: none. Darnand remains skeptical when confronted with matters artistic, behind which too often lies concealed: the Jew—he'll say no more about that. Total incapacity to comprehend the beauties of philosophy or metaphysics. As an adult he encounters enormous difficulty learning by heart words such as *Kriegsverwaltungschef* or *Oberkriegsverwaltungsrat*. He gets round this difficulty by screaming *Heil* each time he encounters one of these remarkable words.

Limited intellectual resources, therefore, but considerable aptitude for administering both physical and mental forms of torture: this activity thrills him. Darnand, alas, is the boss, a boss is a boss, you can't fuck with that, as it is his custom to declare (he's fond of tautology); a boss cannot monopolize every pleasure, however, and must resign himself to leaving some scraps for his subordinates; for every job merits a salary, as it is his custom to declare (he's fond of proverbs); salary and reward, as it is his custom to add, for Darnand is not ungrateful and knows how to reward his boys when they have worked hard: the bone of a resistance fighter, for example, or failing that, of something else.

Mama, I cried out, offended. It was all I was able to say. It wasn't much.

He makes immoderate use of the words *honor* and *dishonor*. Like every crook. Or every military man. We'll leave it up to the jurors to decide which.

The founder of a militia of murderers whose ferocity was often reflected in their faces, Darnand and his big balls . . .

Mama, please, I exclaimed. I was well past the point at which one feels shame, if such a thing is to be imagined. I

28

explained to the process-server that my mother's vulgarity was in a sense ontological, and also astoundingly resistant to neuroleptic drugs. Mama is a case of scientific interest, I repeated to him. Her doctor, Dr Logos, what a name, my God, Dr Logos repeats this to me quite often.

Darnand recruits poor devils, Mama rambled on, or rather devils who happen to be poor and who, were it not for the events of which we speak, would have become perfectly peaceable pimps, second-rate leisure-loving crooks, small-time inner-city drug-dealing big-shots, instead of which! They sure were out of luck! Darnand selects his recruits, whom he calls "my boys," in accordance with a number of strict criteria: they must know how to kill like a hunter and obey like a hound: two qualities that, in the higher mammals, are rarely found to coexist. At your command, they roar, the instant they're told to commit some vile atrocity. I shall omit to describe them, my dear, I have no desire whatever to see you faint. They scour the village in a ludicrous outfit: baggy trousers and a beret crushed like a cow chip on their flat heads, like a big cow chip, my mother said, like the kind of big cow chip that attracts flies, my mother said, but that somehow doesn't make anyone feel like laughing, not in the slightest, she said, and she stopped short.

Come to think of it, what have you done with your beret? she cried out, turning toward the process-server who was examining from every angle the horrible ornamental cabinet that Grandmother had left us. And she started laughing, and it seemed she'd never stop, because her madness exacerbated her every mood, and I laughed along with her, standing there in front of the process-server, who for his part remained as impassive as a statue.

I must explain, I said to the process-server, once I had sti-
fled my nervous giggling, that Mama has focussed much of her
hatred for Darnand and his brutes on the berets they wore. In
Mama's view, the beret is a metonymic object, I said earnestly,
the ugliness of the detail denotes the ugliness of the whole:
for under ordinary circumstances, even external ugliness is
sometimes not easy to determine, while the internal variety is
even harder. The beret, she argues, is the anti-erotic object *par
excellence*: it is what sets base souls apart. Any human being,
she insists, adorned with such a device must at once be deemed
suspect. One need only cite Franco, Saddam Hussein, Monsieur Cousinet from floor five, and that unspeakable Wagner, to
mention but the best known, all of them hideous, all loathsome,
and all of them devotees of the abominable cow chip.

For those who, my mother said, floored by my daughter's
dazzling demonstration, no longer know what to wear on their
heads—but whom was she addressing?—I have listed a great
variety: the simple cap, either fringed or with a bobble; the
fez; the woolen or fur pillbox hat; the balaclava; the sombrero;
the Borsalino; the leather, woolen, or cotton cap, whether
plain, polka-dotted, checked, or floral, very becoming if, like
my Louisiane, you wear it with its peak pulled down at the
back; the hood and I'll skip the rest: as you can see, there is
no lack of choice.

His boys, I was saying, my mother said, are excessively
male. Their beards are rough, their fingers callous. They never
admit they're tired and, if they experience a weakness in the
legs, a shot of liquor, for Christ's sake, and they're back on top,
no bullshit. They walk with a swagger, a knife nudging their
fly. Fleecy down trembles at the tops of their open shirts. How
exciting it is! Everywhere they go, they arouse the passions of

so-called housewives who go crazy at their booming voices, their nicely packaged balls and their boorish manners.

Mama! I said. But my mother had long ago learned to exploit to the full the immunity that was granted her because of her health status and she was not, I feared, remotely inclined to curtail her peroration.

In sexual as well as in military matters, these brutes mount an assault, take up position, then do the job, pure and simple. They're not satisfied until they've knocked down their opponent and ripped off her panties without further ado. Afterwards they quickly do up their fly. The girl, whom they haven't taken the trouble to undress, lies sobbing on the bed, because love has begun to take root in her tender heart, and these swaggering brutes are delighted to see her shedding tears of true love on their account. But as they leave, the unhappy girl timidly murmurs a few words that just might be interpreted as a reproach. That's all they goddamn need. For this slut to create a scene. What nerve! She's had her squirt, so what's she complaining about? She didn't flinch at being screwed, she's not going to get all romantic now, the little whore.

The girl, upset at being treated like a dog, now stammers out some harsher reproaches. She deserves a couple of slaps, the boy thinks as he readjusts his trousers, anyway that's what she's expecting, the whore, a good beating. But he has other cats to whip. He prefers to leave. He feels the blade of his knife against his thigh recalling him to his work. I got things to do, bye. And as he kicks the door shut, Good riddance, the girl cries out with the phony cynicism of those who are young and desperate, for this girl is indeed desperate, she has given away her most prized possession and this is all she has to show for it: she's really been had.

Then comes for this brute the truly orgasmic moment when he is able to boast of his prowess to his friends and describe in great detail the defects of the waitress who received him with patriotic enthusiasm, her flabby tits, her equally flabby ass, her yellow pubic hair, but oh! how she rode me, Christ, what a volcano, fucking shit, talk about hot, they should have seen how he shafted her, the slut, busting his nuts, fucking Christ, all the way up to her uvula, fucking shit, hell what a slut, what a slut! Thus purged, the spirit of the male can now devote itself to what, above all else, is most dear to him: his love for his boss. For all torturers, Mama declared, are always driven by their love for their boss. It's the rule.

These vile braggarts, my mother went on, bursting into a wretched laugh that made her walrus belly and the hideous fanny pack that girdled it leap and flap, every one of these tough guys has his heart set on ending his little life as a little shopkeeper, with a little car, a little wife, and four little kiddies over whom he will rule with an iron hand, for Christ's sake, because a father is due some respect, holy shit, a damned good beating by way of example from time to time, just to set things straight, fucking shit, you can't dick around with your brats' education, there's things you can't ignore, and if you didn't control yourself, there are times you could really do them . . .

All killers dream of respectability, my mother said, it's really quite curious. They dream of enjoying, some day soon, the esteem of their village notables who have until now held them in the greatest contempt. But the notables of their village will never ever, do you understand, my dear, grant them this satisfaction, because never mind how powerful or feared they become, they will never be part of the same world. The great things, Epicurus wrote, are the ones you cannot purchase. It's a maxim, my dear, that I repeat to myself every time I open the refrigerator.

Mama, you'll exhaust yourself, I suggested feebly. But, when it came to spewing out her nonsense, Mama was inexhausible.

Darnand, their gang leader, she resumed after lighting a cigarette, Darnand experiences intense tenderness when reminiscing about the garrison, haricot bean stew and the smell of cold farts in the barracks. He too farts silently and murderously whenever he feels the need, but never on his life before a German officer, because the German does not fart, Mama observed, for the German is a monster, she said.

Mama, I stuttered, blushing with shame.

After coffee washed down with cognac, Darnand likes to sing barracks-room songs like *Tiens voilà du boudin* or *La Madelon*. He knows every verse by heart. Because basically he's a jovial fellow. Jovial, that's the word I was looking for, my mother rejoiced.

There are several words that sound patriotic to his musical ears. These words are pussy, pubis, pastis, patriot, prick, purge, puke, and poke. I'm afraid the list may not be exhaustive.

My mother's coarseness, I mumbled by way of excuse to the impassive process-server who was now engaged in a painstaking examination of the contents of the horrible ornamental cabinet, my mother's coarseness only erupts, you see, under the combined impact of insomnia and sorrow, so do not be offended by it. My mother, in spite of her ways, is a harmless woman, a little lamb, Mr Process-Server, moreover she only screams to disguise her fear, that's what I've come to understand. Right now, for example, Mr Process-Server, my mother is afraid of you, I know her, she must be wondering who you are, are you perhaps a killer? the murderer of her Jean? With my mother, fear consists of everything that she can imagine and the fact is that she endlessly imagines that at every moment the very worst possible thing is taking place. So my mother is afraid of everything, Monsieur, my mother is afraid of everything, even of God whom sometimes in her delirium she calls Putain, she is afraid of me her daughter, afraid of herself, afraid of everything, as if all the fears in the world had been gathered together within her and had been blown up to unprecedented proportions.

And my mother, I was thinking, has filled me with this fear. I'm afraid of men, I'm afraid of the night when ghosts are out, I'm even afraid of Marshal Pétain whom my mother believes to be alive, I'm afraid of noises and of what's outdoors. I'm so afraid that I live barricaded in this lousy apartment that nobody ever enters, locked into a tête-à-tête with a mother who considers herself the widow of a brother who has been dead more than fifty years; a mother who is inconsolable and, as if that weren't enough, insane, and whom I am obliged to treat accordingly, which is to say badly, which is to say by keeping her penned in, which is to say by bludgeoning her with drugs, but what else am I to do? a mother who wakes me up each night screaming, Why, Why? Why what? I ask her from the depths of my slumber. And my dreams answer me but I cannot understand them. A mother of whom I'm ashamed and whom I hide from everyone, even from Nelly, I'm so sick of it; a mother whose illness I keep secret as if keeping it secret could somehow magically take it away, but it's the opposite that happens; a mother who claims she is not grieving for one person but for the whole of humanity, you get the picture, and who spends her days disinterring memories that reek of death. Couldn't you just file your memories away somewhere and forget about them? I say to her. But no, my mother can't, Mr Process-Server, because her memory of terror follows her around like a bitch licking at her legs. A mother that I have to watch over like a child, do this, do that, sleep, calm down; a mother that I feed, that I punish both as a matter of principle and for the sake of revenge, I'll explain what I mean later, whom I protect against Darnand's Militia who harass her at night and who wake her up by kicking her in the stomach: for my mother is my daughter, Mr Process-Server, my mother is my daughter forty years older than myself, and I have to raise her. I could do without this, believe me.

I'm afraid of everything, I'm afraid of rats, spiders, and above all else snakes, and I think I would die on the spot if one of those Arabs from Place Jema el-Fna whom Jawad told me about, wound a rattlesnake around my neck, with its cold, viscous skin. Just yesterday I was confiding to Nelly that sometimes I dreamt of a long snake silently slithering its way into my bed and then choking me in hideous pain. And Nelly replied with her customary brutality, The snake, it's a cock. To which I countered that although I was utterly inexperienced in the affairs of Venus, a cock that zigzags and loops itself like a piece of spaghetti, forget it!

I'm afraid of everything, afraid of the process-server who stands before me with his briefcase and his ugly face, and I have to admit that I'm afraid of my mother when she stares at me without recognizing me, as happens more and more often, when she stares at me with her crazy eyes, with her eyes that accuse me of a crime I haven't committed, and then I find myself obliged to tell her, It's me, Louisiane, your daughter,

Mama don't be frightened, it's me, don't be scared, for at times I dread that in her ravings she might mistake me for Corinne Luchaire or some other such bitch and lash out at me.

But my mother at that precise moment mistook me for neither Corinne Luchaire nor Eva Braun. She prolonged the lecture she was giving me in order to educate me, that's what she was forever drumming into me, I'm teaching you History because soon I shall die, the mouths of the last survivors will be filled with earth, and who will there be to tell you of the paralipomena of the dying century? The parali-what? All these horrors, my dear, that shout out to us from this earth. But all I was asking for was just one thing, that she should never again speak to me of Darnand, or Putain, or any of those other bastards. The stories of the good old days that systematically ended up with six million murdered, thank you very much, I've had my fill. It's simple: the only stories I like are about unrequited love.

Darnand, my mother resumed, thanks to his criminal ideas, which in 1943 were very much in fashion, is appointed Chief of Police. His lawful wife, which is to say the one woman whom he never fucks at all, cries for joy when he swears allegiance to Putain. When he is appointed honorary member of the Waffen-SS with the rank of *Sturmbannführer*, his wife, a decidedly sensitive soul, heaves great sobs, how handsome he is, how strong, what masculine energy emanates from his sweaty body, and those medals on his chest, what a pretty sight! Darnand in an SS uniform swears allegiance to the Führer and pledges him his and obedience unto death. His spouse starts to sob again when her husband repeats to her the words of Ribbentrop: I rejoice infinitely to have made the acquaintance of a man who agrees one hundred percent with German ideas.

Darnand declares that he is ready to rot for the moth-
erland, excuse me, my mother said, I meant to *die* for the
fatherland.* There is just one argument for the defense of the
fatherland: murder; just one method: murder. Results guaranteed. By virtue of its remarkable simplicity, this political
system is destined, in line with the universal principle that
humankind despises thought as a constant source of uncer-
tainties and hairsplitting, this system, I was saying, is destined
to seduce the greatest number.

If you would like to put the finishing touches to this portrait of your leader, my mother said to the process-server, now
is the moment.

Now is the moment, I interjected just as dryly, for you,
Mama, to go to bed.

My mother gave me a frightened look and made a move
toward her room.

At home, Mr Process-Server, it is I who am in command,
as you will have realized. I control the finances, which in fact
consist of the 3,000 francs a month of my mother's disabil-
ity pension. I'm in charge of the checkbook. I run things. I
administrate. I supervise. I do the adding up. And, above all,
the taking away. All of which is extremely hard on the nervous system. Because if Mama sticks her nose in, it's chaos,
I'm being polite. And so, Mr Process-Server, I *drive* her, as
they say in English. I have no option. You ask yourself, does
this burden weigh heavily on my frail shoulders? To be perfectly frank: no, it does not. Having Mama under my command gives me a pleasure I won't hide. I have, I believe, some

---

* Here, presumably deliberately, Rose Mélie creates a spoonerism, which
I am afraid has defeated translation. What Rose Mélie first says is *pourrir
pour la matrie*; she then corrects this to *mourir pour la patrie*.

small talent for despotism. And I take pride in it. It's a gift that constitutes, I have been told, one of the most positive factors in the struggle for social advancement, Christ! I'm talking like Monsieur Cousinet from floor five, for the way is narrow, as our aforementioned neighbor warns, and the number of those chosen for such advancement is few. But I only know how to exercise my despotic talents to the detriment of my mother. Which is regrettable. Do you think, Mr Process-Server, that I could mend my ways? I fervently hope so.

The process-server, who possessed a notable sense of reserve, raised his small, expressionless eyes to look at me. And in that cold, impersonal and droning tone that seemed to me the height of distinction—no doubt because it was the opposite of our own sometimes plaintive, often shrill, always exaggerated and dramatic tone—he inquired, In what year was your television set manufactured? as he readjusted his gilt-framed spectacles.

SIX

The previous day, I had for a moment considered hiding the TV at Nelly's. It was essential that it escape the inventory. Then I had thought better of it. I couldn't carry such a heavy appliance all by myself.

I spent part of that evening dreaming of some kind of miraculous event, a disaster that might enable me to forestall my own disaster: our housing project would collapse but I would escape unharmed, an earthquake, a massive flood would come and sweep everything away, the process-server, his seizure order, his briefcase filled with threats, and my mother as well. For I could not prevent myself from interpreting the announced arrival of this process-server as a dire warning, a sort of punishment visited upon us for our somewhat unique, not to say utterly deranged, mode of living.

I had a hard time getting to sleep, so I settled myself comfortably on my pillow in my favorite position, one hand resting on the TV remote, the other on my groin. What would happen to us, I said to myself, if after the seizure we were evicted, what would I do with this old madwoman?

I shouldn't think about tomorrow, I said to myself. The moment I think about tomorrow, I see a tide bearing me off toward something black and cold that I cannot picture, except in the form of a gigantic squid, which is absurd. I shouldn't think of the future which, according to the most optimistic predictions, promises to be grim. And I shouldn't think of the past, which, if I'm to believe my mother, was a nightmare. So what exactly can I think about? I wondered aloud. I'm having big problems at the factory, complained the man in the night-blue suit in the show on the TV that I had just turned on. You just can't understand, he shouted at the deferential woman with the fashionable hairstyle—these two attributes seeming to me, for whatever obscure reason, to go together in people of the female sex—who was standing opposite him. The man wore a superior grin on his face and he emphasized each syllable with a nod of his head in an attempt to give to his gestures the conviction that his soul so cruelly lacked. I do understand, murmured the woman who, as I have said, had just had her hair impeccably blow-dried. And with no other prolegomena, the two heads of the impeccably hairstyled couple bent and exchanged a kiss that the camera operator had, stupidly, filmed from behind.

I always examine with particularly close attention the different kinds of film kisses. My curiosity about them is, I admit, extreme. I always examine with passionate interest whether the actor's kiss is placed to one side of, above or below, the mouth of the actress—as is, and I deplore the fact, frequent—and whether the kiss consists in simple mouth-to-mouth contact (entailing different degrees of pressure, suction, adhesiveness, and hygrometry) or whether it is accompanied by the protrusion of the tongue as in the kiss that Jack Nicholson administers to Jessica Lange in *The Postman Always Rings Twice* or the one I observed recently in *Trainspotting*, these wholly exceptional kisses being indisputably the most interesting.

But the spell was broken, because the man in the night-blue suit didn't know how to pursue his advantage vis-à-vis the neck of the woman with the blow-dried hair or vis-à-vis her breasts which were, it seems to me, most noteworthy. The man in the night-blue suit and the woman with the blow-dried hair disentwined quickly, as if they were in a hurry to be done with it, in spite of the fact that the series' plot might incline one to believe quite the opposite: to get over his split from Pattie, the love of his life, Danver throws himself headlong into his work, which is how he meets Diana, the sister of Sammy, his main rival within the firm. Sammy will go to any length to prevent Diana from falling in love with Danver, Christ! it's straight out of Racine. What is going to happen when Sammy stumbles upon Danver and Diana in the middle of a passionate kiss?

In this connection, I note, not without annoyance, that film kisses are often performed at a gallop, if I may express it like that, and consequently leave the viewer thirsting for more. Which is truly irritating. For, it cannot be denied that film kisses, observed at evening's end, when the numbed spirit craves its own annihilation, are a real consolation, the merited reward for an interminable day, its crowning, I'd even say its apotheosis, provided however that these kisses are slow, slow, slow, with an ardent, fervent slowness, slow, slow, slow and long and languorous and languid and liquid and lascivious and *linguae* if possible, and lyrical of course and they must leave one troubled, tottering, all atremble.

Film kisses possess, when compared with real-life kisses, a certain number of advantages: they don't muss up your hair, don't make powdered cheeks blush, don't leave lipstick smears all around your mouth, which is ugly and, I might as well tell it like it is, grotesque, and above all, they don't twist faces into frightful grimaces at the very moment when they should be radiating the sublimely, divinely transfiguring light of love.

Nonetheless, I return to this subject because it appears to me to be of some importance: film kisses disappoint more often than not because they're brief and botched, not to say expeditious, that's the reproach I level at them, and, I note this in passing, they certainly hurt ratings, what a waste! whereas Nelly and Jawad's kisses, to cite but one example, can last an hour and thirty-five minutes, right through a film, and even longer. Where was I? Kisses led me astray. Ah yes, the couple with the fashionable hairstyles, I was saying, loosened its clinch and the woman started reeling off her nonsense again as though the kiss had modified nothing within her deepest being, no alteration could be read in her face, she had the same placid voice as before and, in spite of her make-up, the same air of oafish stupidity, you could not detect in her that sweet languor that hangs on every gesture like the weight of too great a happiness, nor did her gaze shine with that strange sparkle I have observed in Nelly's eyes when she draws away from Jawad, and which is like the sparkle of laughter without the laughter that customarily escorts it, I'm talking ravishingly.

I therefore deduced that the actors had exchanged nothing but a fake kiss. Those idiots had failed to make the most of a golden opportunity. No doubt they were married. Most likely their spouses were both rather old-fashioned and life in Hollywood had not yet made them blasé, and they were constantly watching them out of the corners of their eyes, gripped by the most fanatical jealousy.

Before falling asleep, my thoughts again returned to the seizure notice I had received two days before. I kept repeating to myself that I must at all costs get into the appointed process-server's good graces in order to weaken him, to circumvent him and to persuade him to postpone his deadline or, better still, to cancel it altogether. In my credulity, in my foolishness, I ought to say, I considerably overestimated the powers of a process-server. I consequently resolved to show him around our abode with an accompaniment of carefully chosen expressions, exquisite pleasantries and lively patter respecting all the treacherous rules of past-participle agreement, my weak point in grammar. It wasn't until much later that I realized that all such attentions were not only futile but ridiculous, and that the only things likely to impress such beings as this process-server were neither the moronic smiles nor the bowing and scraping with which, as we shall see, I was to exhaust myself, but rather haughtiness and disdain. And spite.

Do you remember the purchase date? repeated the process-server, still stationed, as straight as the letter i, in front of the television.

I summoned up my courage. On no account did I wish to surrender a device that allowed me to make a scientific examination not only of the kiss in all its multiple forms but also of various other sexual behaviors which, in spite of the numerous efforts that I had made to gain instruction, remained totally enigmatic to me. (I happen to possess some very marked libidinous tendencies and the contrast between the impetuosity of the said tendencies and their utter lack of exercise is a source of infinite suffering to me.)

Mr Process-Server, it seems to me advisable to warn you that the seizure of that TV set may well catapult my mother into the worst possible nightmare—my audacity astounded me—for that everyday apparatus, I said, pointing a professorial finger at the TV, exerts on Mama's mutilated mind a veritable prophylactic effect, I would go so far as to say a fortifying and regenerative effect, which is not to be disregarded. In such adverse circumstances, I thought, a little blackmail could do no harm. I therefore pointed out to him the many advantageous effects that the presence of such a medicine could have upon my mother. The fact is that it enables her, I argued, to engage in long conversations with the screen, which ease her sick brain, conversations which are far preferable to those we hold together, since these latter are marked by mutual and insurmountable incomprehension.

Furthermore, I said, for my mother who has come to regard leaving her home as degrading, for my mother who, since the assassination of Bousquet, has become the enemy of all society, perhaps you don't understand what the assassination of Bousquet has to do with this? I'll come back to that! for my mother who accordingly lives holed up in her bedroom as in a bunker, the TV provides the assurance that the world exists and that it continues to rot. Given its immaterial and chimerical nature, this may constitute a paradox, yet television, Mr Process-Server, affords my mother a stable counterpoint to reality, I don't know if I'm making myself understood, it is like a lighthouse in the dark night of her mind (I have a weakness for poetic images, however hard I struggle), a terrestrial landmark that is guaranteed, permanent and almost invariable from one day to the next (the same vile pap dished out every day, I inwardly corrected) to which she clings in order to ward off vertigo and the urge to leap into the empty void toward which her soul is inexorably drawn.

But, at times, my mother who has this ability to change her opinion (as easily as if it were a shirt, I was about to remark stupidly), and also to embrace several conflicting thoughts at once, my mother, I was saying, begins at times to doubt the reality of the world she observes on the screen. It seems to me, my dear, she confides to me, that this world doesn't really exist. It seems to me it's just a soap opera with a cast of nothing but extras shot in a studio as vast as the earth itself by an abominable director, Putain perhaps, or Darnand, or some other pig of the same type or, worse still, by a hidden and diabolical power about which no one can do anything, an authority or a God-knows-what that has a terrible weakness for action films with deaths, wars, devastation, blood everywhere, and stunts.

Mama says this director regularly engages veteran psychiatrists to restore the morale of the extras who are paid next to nothing and who are dressed up, as need dictates, as warriors, beggars, victims, killers, and whatever else is desired, which proves in the long run a rather demoralizing activity and sometimes requires the actors to take Prozac. These extras even go, my mother claims—she is completely nuts—even go so far as to act out their own deaths on fake war fronts while an army officer, the spitting image of General Lammerding, presents their weeping widows with a nickel medal and a check for 15,000 francs.

What is more, I said to the process-server who, not obtaining from me the hoped-for reaction, was examining with meticulous care the lamp that stood on the dresser and, with a frown, was jotting in his notebook: a lamp consisting of an imitation-wood stand in the form of a vine stock topped with a yellow cardboard lampshade scorched on one side, what is more, Mama asserts that television opens her up to the Universal, an entity with which she is infinitely enchanted. For, as she sits before this animated rectangular thing, Mama senses that she is but a small particle of the Great Whole and that she is melting body and soul into Universal Love. Mama believes in that great joke, I said sarcastically (sarcasm calmed my nerves), above all when she watches those soft-porn TV movies broadcast late at night on M6, those third-rate orgies, those third-rate oral-sex scenes amid third-rate interior decor, yet I can't help thinking: shouldn't lust be more luxurious? I'm straying from the point, I'm straying, I beg you to excuse me. Where was I? Universal Love. Mama believes in its existence with all her soul, Monsieur, and does so despite the fact that the cruelest proofs of its nonexistence are inflicted upon her daily. For my mother, I said with irony, is deadly romantic, which is something, it seems to me, that cannot be cured by traditional forms of medicine. For my mother cannot get enough of the union of sensitive souls, the perfect harmony of love and other such gooey confections. And little does it trouble her that inside her head these repulsive notions wage a vicious civil war with her equally peremptory conceptions regarding the hideousness of men in general and of Putain in particular, because, you see, her romantic soul is wildly in love with strife, and not only does she love it, she provokes and encourages it. It's hell.

I might add, I said with conviction, for in truth it was my own cause that I was now cunningly pleading, I might add that her very personal interpretation of what she sees on TV encourages and feeds her reflection on major transcendental issues. TV corroborates her ways of seeing, her *ways of raving* might be more accurate, and reinforces the foundations of her tottering theories, her moonshine stories, Mr Process-Server, that Putain did this, that Darnand did that, that's her obsession, that the civil war is just beginning and that ideas trafficking, just like arms trafficking, is run by the international mafia of collaborationists who maintain tight control over the industries of emptiness which, she maintains, are booming: always the same litanies, Mr Process-Server, in the end I take no notice. But it is my duty to note that these speculations, though far-fetched, have the gift of calming my mother down as effectively as Tranxene. From which I infer, I said with an air of competence, that, counter to popular belief, thinking tranquilizes.

I shall not, Mr Process-Server, beat about the bush, my self-possession astonished me, so I'll just say by way of conclusion that this instrument which you're trying most wickedly to confiscate, is necessary to my Mama since it enlightens her, tranquilizes her, inspires her, and nourishes her natural eloquence and lyricism. For all of these reasons and others which I cannot here relate, you will inflict upon her, if you take away this TV set—which for her is nothing less, I repeat, than a prosthesis—you will inflict upon her a most considerable injustice.

To finish, I said (I could have expanded on the subject for days on end but I had the impression I was becoming a bore), just as long as Mama argues with the screen, she leaves me in peace and, believe me, that's not to be sneez . . .

But I hadn't time to complete my sentence, for . . .

. . . for my mother, who had remained silent for a few moments and who I thought had calmed down—but my mother never calmed down, I should have known that from experience—my mother turned back to the process-server, and gazed at him as if awaking from a dream.

What the hell's he doing here, this *milico*?

Monsieur is not a member of the Militia, I said.

Then what is Monsieur? my mother said.

Monsieur is a process-server, I said.

Same thing, my mother said. The mere existence of a process-server is an insult to the ideals of Universal Love that I hold dear.

I, I said . . .

Someone who rapes and violates people's homes, excuse me, but what would you call such a person?

A rapist, I said.

And someone who takes things that don't belong to him?

A thief, I said.

Usually so slow to express myself, for once my mouth had raced ahead of my mind. I had the sudden feeling that I had made a big mistake. Panic took hold of me. My bewildered thoughts fled in all directions. Return to your bed this minute, I screamed, hoping to undo the damage. But the damage was done.

My mother took a few timorous steps toward her bedroom but, just as she was stepping over the threshold, she stopped, seized by a sudden intuition, then spinning round, It's Leducq who's denounced us!

I have to acknowledge that Mama, in her madness, does display astounding wisdom. Leducq is our landlord and we owe him more than seven months' rent, and he's ruthlessly calling in his debts in spite of the dilatory and heartfelt letters with which I bombard him every month.

Where does this acute insight of hers come from? is a question I often ask myself. Probably from her disdain for everyday events, because when it comes to everyday events, my mother couldn't give a damn, you only need take a cursory glance at the pigsty in which she lives to convince yourself of this fact; from her disdain for everyday events combined with the ability of her pineal eye (I like playing with scientific concepts) to penetrate secrets, hidden vices, the whole underbelly of feelings, and to decipher the subtlest of details lurking beneath the jumble of appearances; and it is these two skills that combine to afford her this vision of things stripped of their varnish, as the poet writes, calling varnish what others call shit, a rhetorical technique that is known as transposition.

It's Leducq who's denounced us!

And as if the word denounced had suddenly jump-started her memory, Mama recalled the letter of denunciation she had seen being written at the Café des Platanes fifty-four years earlier, a letter about which she had raved at least a hundred times and which in her eyes was at the heart of the family misfortune, a misfortune handed down all the way to us and which, were I to judge by the present conjuncture of events, remained extremely active. Do you think, Mr Process-Server, that misfortune can be inherited?

Mama saw again the smoke-filled café where her mother, my grandmother, loved to go when her fingers were weary from too much sewing, she saw again the wooden tables huddled around the stove, the pensioners playing their ritual game of belote with the seriousness of court clerks under the gaze of Marshal Pétain whose duly framed portrait enjoyed pride of place over the counter between the liquor license and a poster that had read DUCO DUCON DUCONNET ever since the café owner, a highly facetious soul, as will be explained later, with three strokes of his paintbrush, had turned the stuttering *B*s of the famous French aperitif, Dubonnet, into stuttering *C*s, thereby producing a climactic play on the French for "cunt." She saw again the face of her mother as she read *Le Petit Écho de la Mode*, while remaining nonetheless alert to the discussions of the men, since it was these discussions, punctuated as they were by filthy jokes and loud goddamns, that taught her about the world, its undreamed-of dimensions, its geography, its colors and the oh-so-beautiful names of its capital cities. This, my dear, my mother said, is how your grandmother discovered the existence of Narvik and of Mers el-Kébir, this is how she learned that the word "pussy" had no fewer than thirty-six synonyms, that women in Russia all have beards, incredible! that Scotsmen on Sundays dress up as majorettes, even process-servers? even process-servers! and tax-collectors? same thing! no kidding! I'm telling you! And that a large proportion of Americans, commonly referred to as *Amerloques*, consisted of Negroes, vulgarly referred to as *niggers*, *spades*, or *baboons*, the resemblance with these latter creatures being so striking that at times they might even be confused.

While I played dominoes with the son of the café owner, my mother said, her gaze fixed straight ahead of her, the hardware-store owner and the sexton laconically discussed the changes that had come to pass within the High Unattainable Spheres. They're only interested in one thing and that's this stuff! the sexton declared, giving himself a resounding thump on the chest at the supposed location of his wallet, Right here! he said, landing himself a further thump on the chest that made him stagger, "pack up your troubles . . . and smile, smile, smile." Maurice Chevalier sang on the radio, Oh how we are spoiled, my grandmother read, hot on the heels of the talented Maggy Rouff along comes Madame Lanvin, one of the goddesses of Parisian haute couture, who is presenting her latest creations, which before long all the women of Paris will be wearing. His elbows on the bar, the bicycle dealer was telling the café owner, who wasn't listening to him but kept gently nodding his head to pretend he was, the bicycle dealer, I can still see him, was telling him that at the wedding of Duteuil's daughter some practical joker had put mustard in one of the sections of the cake, and who had ended up with the mustardy slice? Who? Who? You'll never guess in a thousand years! Old Piche! You should have seen her face! Priceless! said the bicycle dealer, bursting into laughter to prove how amusing it was; and your grandmother, my dear, who had listened to his story absentmindedly while skimming through an article on Suzy Solidor's latest romantic idyll, your grandmother let out a friendly little laugh, for she possessed such tact, the indubitable hallmark of great souls.

Larzillière and Desmottes returned for the umpteenth time to the subject of the white slave trade, which was controlled, they had this on good authority, by scheming, flesh-eating, hook-nosed Jews who stole all their money from the French and dispatched young and pure-of-soul city girls to Amsterdam and thence to the nether districts of Bamako to perform blow-jobs for ghastly Negroes hung like mules. Lord Jesus, the priest exclaimed. Well, these men have got to dream, your grandmother thought, seeing in the disheveled rantings of Larzillière and Desmottes nothing other than the unbridled sexual phantasmagoria of unsatisfied men who had never been out into the big bad world and who knew nothing of love but the statutory sad embrace accorded once a month by an ugly, acrimonious, and perpetually ill-tempered wife.

Listening for the hundredth time to the repellent memories of my mother—are there any memories that do not repel? if so, I'd like to be told—I had a sudden urge to run away and to forget about the whole thing, my mother, her Putain, the process-server, and his briefcase. It's an idea that often worked its way into my mind, to run far away from my mother and her ghosts that, strangely, had become my ghosts too, and settle in the Oise valley in the company of dumb and peace-loving animals. I glanced at the door, at my mother, at the door, at my mother, at the door. I felt thrilled at the possibility, repented, felt scared, pulled myself together, abandoned the idea. In exactly that order.

While one of the four pensioners, my mother was saying, caught up in her memories, called out trump ta-trump! and ten bonus points! as he slammed down a ten of spades, Marcon, not to feel left out, emphatically advised the gathered company to avoid drinking fizzy drinks since Jews were known to lace them with invisible diamond powder which then severed the fibers of the intestines and in two seconds flat landed you in the cemetery.

That's garbage, remarked Larzillière, who was nobody's fool.

Total crap, echoed the café owner, eager to prevent liquor consumption dropping even a milliliter.

In fact, at the Café des Platanes conversations about Jews soon ran out of steam. They lacked, in a manner of speaking, fuel, my mother said. For Desmottes, Larzillière, and Marcon had nobody within their sights with whom they might compare the horrible faces contorted by lust and greed that filled the leaflets that the mayor's office circulated to all businesses and public buildings. These dreadful images, these hairy, animal faces had no more reality in their eyes than the cardboard cutout monsters they had seen in horror films at the Novelty Theater, they had no connection with anything they knew or could identify and so, unable to assume any known fleshly form, they dissolved in alcohol.

Do you have the invoice for this radio set? the process-server demanded as he picked up the radio that I'd bought myself for my seventeenth birthday.

Since you ask, Inspector, said Mama (she called him Inspector!), I shall answer you very frankly that my mother, then so different from the person she was later to become, my mother in those days tended not to get particularly indignant about the outrages she overheard. For in her view such horrors were nothing more than a harmless exercise, a propaedeutic in which the word Jew designated nothing but thieves, bums, cowards, whether they were Jews, Gypsies, or Venerquois, a sort of prelude paving the way to broader metaphysical inquiries. (Later, she reproached herself most bitterly for not having reacted to these odious declarations in the way that she should have done.)

The best thing, I recommended to the process-server who, having read the invoice, was now jotting down in his notebook: a Panasonic stereophonic radio-cassette player, peak power 80 watts, CD player with 36 programmable tracks, digital tuner, measuring 45x19x26 cm, purchase date December 8, 1996, the best thing is to give my mother's outpourings a free rein. The liberal approach has proved, in her case, to be the most effective: letting her ramble, not being rough with her, while granting her the illusion that she is free. Mama always ends up wearing herself out on her own. The main thing is to be patient. It is apparently rumored in financial circles that there is no resistance that does not yield with time, and that one day or the next every revolution runs out of steam of its own accord. Do you concur with this view?

The process-server remained silent. The capacity of this man for not reacting was worthy of admiration, comparable (and this is no mean feat) to that of Dr Logos.

Let's reserve for later, I said in a low voice, the standard methods of coercion and intimidation. I can state from experience that there are few occasions on which I have to resort to such extremes. I was speaking as a specialist. I had become one. You fear perhaps that all of this will make you lose time? But what *is* losing time? And what *is* gaining it? Isn't gaining time, all things considered, the same as losing it? I said this in a sudden surge of lyricism that I immediately regretted.

Now, my mother recalled, Desmottes and Larzillière were raising their voices because the conversation had turned to those bastard communists who had this special characteristic whereby you couldn't identify them by their facial features and in fact they could look like anyone at all, Holy Virgin!

cried the priest making the sign of the cross. Anyone at all, Desmottes repeated, you, me—now he was really getting carried away—were it not for their assassin's leer, their blood-smeared butcher's hands, and the knife they gripped between their ferocious teeth.

Larzillière and Desmottes then cast their minds back to the revolutionary hotheads who had distinguished themselves in 1936, Raymond, Brousse, Colin, and a fanatic called Baysse, who taught Spanish at the junior high-school in Auterive: a goddamn poet, the cycle-dealer said, a Maquisard, Larzillière raged, a terrorist financed by the Jews of Moscow, Desmottes screamed.

In order to reduce my mother to silence the use of more convincing arguments, I murmured to the process-server, should not however be ruled out: a blow to the head with the phone book, a punch to the liver or hypogastrium, tying up, gagging—like many people Mama responds to the language of power—or better still: the quick intervention of a psychiatrist, I would tend toward this solution, which is, how can I put it? more elegant. But before reaching this point and triggering events that may prove uncontrollable, perhaps we might be patient a little while longer?

Things were hotting up, Mama said, oblivious to the drama playing out between our own four walls. The white wine was making the men's voices hoarse and inflaming their patriotic sentiments. And every discussion flared with rage against the traitors to the nation.

They have to be killed, cried out Larzillière, who always got nasty after a few drinks. A bullet in the back of the head and that's it!, he yelled, aiming at the door an imaginary shotgun, making the men who were playing belote jump, not that

that prevented them from continuing to play their game with unwavering seriousness.

They all have to be killed, with no exceptions, Desmottes roared as he stubbed out his cigarette with a vindictive hand.

Every last one of them, yelled the municipal policeman, who for a while now had been trying to make a favorable impression on Desmottes and Larzillière. Come on, it's my round, he yelled, as he lurched to the bar. The very best of health to the asshole who's paying! No doubt he was referring to the health of his soul, Mama said, given that that of his body had long ago been dissipated in *eau de vie*.

The process-server, whose face remained so expression-less that it was quite impossible to tell whether or not he was listening to my mother, now approached the living-room coffee table, bent down over it, felt it with sweaty fingers that left a mark, measured it with a tape measure that he took from his pocket, and wrote in his little notebook: one coffee table 80 cm long by 50 cm wide, What wood is it made of?

The kind that flutes are made of, I said impulsively, trying to make a joke. It was idiotic. I was attempting to come across as genial, witty, and happy to be alive, whereas I was the exact opposite.

You are right to ask, Inspector, my mother said to the process-server. Every detail is important in an affair of this nature, even the most idiotic. The table beneath which the son of the café owner lured me that day, I mean that terrible day when we witnessed the letter of denunciation being written, the table beneath which he lured me was an ordinary plank table wedged into the storeroom between crates of beer and lemonade and on which walnuts and fruit had been laid to dry for the winter. The café owner's son invited me to crouch down. I crouched. I felt I was being moved by a force more powerful than my will. He pulled down my panties. I made no attempt to stop him. Not a word. Feeble, deep inside, as feeble as ever. With the tip of a colored pencil, he began to caress my genitals. As for me, I was more motionless than a tree. And weak, deathly weak. He continued with his strange caresses. We didn't take our eyes off one other. He opened his fly. Touch me. I touched him. It gave me a funny feeling, neither pleasant nor unpleasant, I don't know how to put it, said Mama addressing the process-server who was continuing his inventory of our bric-a-brac while pretending not to be listening, though I am sure he wasn't missing a word, he had a deceitful, in fact, a downright lecherous air about him.

My mother had her first sexual experience when she was six whereas I, who am eighteen, have never experienced the happiness of being embraced or caressed, this wholly inappropriate thought burst violently into my mind and stuck there for several seconds. My body, I said to myself, has never been churned by the mighty ploughshare of love. (Frustration makes people poetic, as I've observed a thousand times.) As for fucking, I'm totally in the dark. And this lack of experience weighs on me, as though it were a disgrace. I know nothing about it, nothing, just the few rudiments that Nelly has been kind enough to teach me (for her knowledge is considerable), for example that the kisses she administers to Jawad are called blow-jobs, that they are highly nourishing and that they make her wet, that's the word she uses, which, if I've understood correctly, is merely a metaphorical term to signify the liquid nature of desire. But I still have everything to learn about the mechanics of fluidity, hence my interest in film kisses and their hydraulic systems as well as in rubbing, coiling, licking, intromissions, looping, flipping, somersaults, spinning, aerobatics, rockface-assaults, and all the other epileptic performances in which humans, all humans, myself excepted, joyfully indulge.

But that's quite enough of that, I decided, in spite of my longing to feel pity for myself and to brood over my sexual misery, which indeed struck me as absolute.

Conversations about the Communist scum could last entire evenings, Mama resumed, having climbed back aboard her memories, but it was the Jadre twins who railed the most wildly against Communists. Your grandmother, my dear, didn't like the way the Jadre twins spoke of Communists and of the trampled Fatherland. Your grandmother had the feeling that what the Jadre twins were attempting more than anything was to frighten everyone. And the Jadre twins worked hard at it. And excelled at it.

EIGHT

For the Jadre twins barely knew how to read and write but they knew how to frighten people, Mama said.

Sunday afternoons they stride up and down Cours Michelet.

They have their thumbs tucked under their leather belts. They strut.

Their hair is crew cut.

When they pass a group of young girls, they turn around and shout a coarse remark. Then they rock with laughter. They sure know how to have fun!

If they see a dog without an owner, they give it a kick in the stomach. You can't have a dog strolling around without its master. Understood, Fuckhead? they yell at the dog as it runs away howling. It's sidesplitting.

The children watch them, in silence, fascinated.

At the café, they drink. Immoderately. They aren't thirsty but they drink.

They smoke too. A lot. Like me, Mama says. But when they've finished their cigarettes, they don't put them out in the ashtray, they thow them on the floor with an ostentatious flick of their thumb. The café owner's wife can sweep up. Isn't that what she's paid for, for fuck's sake?

When they go to the cinema, they advance down the central aisle without looking either left or right, their genitals prominent (do they stuff their pants with cotton or what?), their thighs wide apart. They advance and, as they advance, silence descends.

Sometimes, after Mass, they shove their begging bowl at us, collecting money in support of Darnand's Militia. They wear a scowl of disdain, conveying thereby that they are not asking for alms, rather, a subtle difference, they are stooping to this work for the combined good of the Fatherland and the Militia. So we throw a coin into their bowl, with a leaden heart, for we would have a thousand times rather kept that coin to purchase some chocolate.

The Jadre twins frighten people and the fear they instill is infinitely pleasing to them.

The Jadre twins frighten the mayor, they frighten the priest, they frighten women, they frighten everybody. But, over time, the people of the village grow accustomed to this fear. Just as they grow accustomed to misfortune. Just as they grow accustomed to horror. And just as they grow accustomed to everything. They, but not I. Not I, Mama cried out, turning toward the process-server who was busy listing the contents of the right-hand drawer of the dresser, including: a key-ring in the shape of a sandal, a Bic ballpoint pen, a photograph dated November 1959 showing my mother behind the items-to-mail counter at the Louvre postal office a few days after being transferred to Paris (one might think she was in a prison visiting-room), a photograph dated March 15, 1979, showing my mother and my father in the courtyard of the Sainte-Anne asylum (although they don't look like lunatics) where they met each other and fell in love, both very briefly, a reel of black thread, some shirt buttons, a Casio-brand wristwatch with a broken strap, a box of matches, a ruler, a multi-function pen-knife, a pair of nail scissors, an envelope containing a letter that Filo wrote in 1943 to Marshal Putain but never sent and which Mama kept as a relic, as well as a heap of papers of no interest.

In the village a lot of things were said regarding the Jadre twins, my mother continued. It was said that as children they used to steal. It was said that their ears were dirty and they smelled of piss. It was said that their mother was a *pute* who got knocked up by a Gypsy or by the village mayor at whose residence she worked as a servant. Versions differed.

Now, Mama said, the Jadre twins are members of the Militia. Their leader said you can take it or leave it: you join us and we'll forget everything. And everything was forgotten.

Now the Jadre twins are proud. It's the first time in their lives that the twins have been proud. They swagger, in their uniforms, guns at their belts.

The Jadre twins are now seeking revenge for their childhoods. Their childhoods that were obliterated! Erased from the map! And woe betide anyone who dares mention them! Just you wait!

The Jadre twins hope that one day soon they'll at last be able to enjoy the esteem of the notables and above all that of the pharmacist whom they pride themselves on calling by his Christian name.

It is to this esteem that they attach the most importance.

For these notables and their fat wives seem to the Jadre twins to be wreathed in extraordinary prestige. They possess, so the twins believe, something extra, a gift, a charm, something that goes beyond mere titles and inheritances, an elegance and a set of manners that the Jadre twins have been denied but shall appropriate at a later date, since everything, it seems, may now be appropriated. But this esteem of which they dream is destined to remain forever beyond the reach of the Jadre twins. Forever, Mama repeated. Because in the eyes of the notables and their fat wives nothing can ever erase the grubby traces of a base origin. Nothing.

The Jadre twins leave the Café des Platanes at six o'clock and make their way to the local headquarters of the Militia, Place Richelme. With them out of the way, one can breathe, Mama murmurs in a dreamy voice, in a completely changed voice, her childhood voice, I thought, her voice from before the disaster, purged of any fear, and all of a sudden I wondered whether, in thirty years time, I in my turn would evoke with the same nostalgic lilt that grim little coffee bar in the shopping mall that I sometimes frequent.

But on the day I'm talking about, Mama said, on the day when the letter of denunciation was written in front of us, a letter which on its own upended an entire world, the café owner came out from behind the counter, of which he constituted the centerpiece and which without him seemed incomplete, and went and sat at a table, near the stove. He was surrounded by Desmottes and Larzillière. When the pharmacist, for whom everyone appeared to have been waiting, pushed open the café door, the café owner lifted his pen to write:

NINE

Venerque, Haute-Garonne, January 12, 1943, Most Venerated *Maréchal* Pétain, We have the honor of drawing your attention to the case of Robert Biron, inhabitant of Venerque, supposedly suffering from rheumatism—r, h, e, u, the pharmacist dictated—from rheumatism, the café owner wrote in a skewed and convoluted hand which somewhat reflected his person, comma, who has been scandalously deemed unfit for compulsory labor service though in fact he possesses a powerful physique and an athletic build—a, t, h, the pharmacist spelled out—and an athletic build, the café owner repeated.

Moreover (in one word, the pharmacist stipulated), moreover, the café owner carefully wrote, we are very surprised that despite the fact that a law has apparently been made to deal with Jews we continue to be taunted every day by a Jewish person. Person's not quite right, the pharmacist declared as he paced up and down, his hands clasped behind his back, oddball, Larzillière suggested, crackpot, Desmottes threw in, let's keep it simple, the pharmacist said: Jew, a one-hundred-per-cent Jew, Larzillière corrected, a one-hundred-per-cent Jew, the café owner wrote. So we ask you: why are there exceptions? It's ironical! Larzillière said. It's ironical, the café owner wrote. We note with bitterness that the laws enacted thanks to your influence serve no purpose, the pharmacist dictated. Not so fast, the café owner said. In my view, Desmottes remarked, that denigrates the Marshal.

Doesn't denigrate him at all, keeps him informed, Larzillière countered.

As we were. This Jew who calls himself Lazarus Apfelbaum, the names they have! Desmottes said, see if he picks up his bed and walks, Larzillière added, ha ha ha, said Larzillière, ha ha ha, said Desmottes, this Jew is the owner of the shirt factory, located in our little commune of Venerque, which he has made the object of a fictitious sale to a dummy purchaser who is only there as an ornament and who, besides, is never seen, never, Larzillière repeated, with the purpose of illegally—two *l*s—illegally evading Aryanization—*r, y*. Full stop. Full stop. He pays his staff very badly. It's a disgrace how badly he pays his staff: they can scarcely survive on their pay.

We would be very grateful to you, eminently, the pharmacist said, we would be very grateful to you eminently, delete the very, the pharmacist said in irritation, do I have to start the whole letter again? the café owner fretted. Don't worry, he'll understand, Desmottes said, if you would be so kind as to verify our assertions and compel him to remunerate his employees at the normal rate.

Concomitantly, concomitantly we advise you that the Spanish teacher of the complementary courses at Auterive, whose name is Baysse, is inculcating our children with skepticism—*s, k*—and the spirit of criticism, which are the two fountainheads that feed and foment trouble, that's nicely expressed, Desmottes acknowledged, nor does he hesitate to make prejudiced comments regarding the decisions of Maréchal Pétain, our venerated Maréchal. He is believed to have Communist pamphlets at his home. It seems to us that it is only right that he be questioned as soon as possible.

Lastly, we inform you that we have asked, requested, said the pharmacist, that we have requested, on behalf of the Tricolor Legion, the cooperation of our little town's well-known singing teacher, Madame Tison, in a Mass in memory of the legionnaires who have died for the honor of France, and that the same Madame Tison has replied, I couldn't give a damn about the Legion. Desmottes couldn't help but giggle. It's not funny, the café owner said, reprovingly. What do you think? Larzillière dictated. What do you think? the café owner copied.

We wish to state, Desmottes dictated, that it is not the informer's spirit that we are displaying (not the informer's spirit that we are displaying, the café owner wrote), what we are displaying is a sense of duty to our country, which we love, Larzillière emphasized, which we love.

How shall we end it? the café owner asked, scratching his head.

You write: "honest Frenchmen," Desmottes said.

Honest Frenchmen, I agree, that's straightforward and decent.

Aren't we going to sign our names? Larzillière fretted.

If we want to get the reward, we have to sign our names, Desmottes confirmed.

We're not doing this for the money, the café owner shouted, shaking with indignation. We're doing this for the Fatherland.

We have to sign our names, the pharmacist declared decisively, not to do so would be cowardice.

The café owner handed the pen to the pharmacist who drew two coiled and pretentious capital letters, then to Desmottes and Larzillière who, with the laborious application of imbeciles, scribbled their spidery scrawls.

And your grandmother who all this time had remained at her table, speechless and seemingly paralyzed, your grandmother, my dear, who didn't want to hear what was being said right in front of her but who could not prevent herself from listening, your grandmother who wanted to shout Stop, stop, but who couldn't get a single sound out, your grandmother who had an angry look on her face that I had never seen before, yanked me by the sleeve and we left the café.

You grandmother was thirty-nine years old. I was six, my mother said.

For my part, I have always had the utmost difficulty imagining that my mother could ever have been six. I am unable to rid myself of the idea that my mother has always been ugly and old and fat. And the idea that I was born from the genitalia of an old woman fills me with infinite disgust. However softly I murmured these words within myself, my mother must have heard them (her soul was telepathic) for she said to me, My childhood, my dear, ended that day.

The most extraordinary thing, I whispered to the process-server who was now making an inventory of the left-hand drawer of the dresser with method, boredom, perspicacity, circumspection, moderation, mistrust, seriousness, composure, carefulness, dignity, placidity, quickness, what have I forgotten? the most extraordinary thing is that my mother's memory, instead of exhausting itself, is growing ever richer and constantly brings forth new recollections. New details appear with each new version of that year of 1943, which was so prodigiously productive of disasters, so that I have the feeling that this history, wherein is mixed a dead brother, a letter of denunciation, and the misdeeds of a Marshal Putain, is nothing but a tissue of lies based on a small number of true events, a history that doesn't exist, that never will exist and in which my mother orders me to believe, a funereal fable which she perfects day in day out, which she embellishes or dramatizes in order to cast herself in an interesting light and to inject into her life the salt, the blood, the sparkle that it has lacked. Does such a hoax strike you as possible, Mr Process-Server? Should I really entertain such a hypothesis?

TEN

I then found myself in the very greatest uncertainty as to the right course to follow. Three options, I counted them, presented themselves to my mind:

ONE—strangle my mother with a table-napkin, finally putting an end to her mythomania, then disguise the crime as a sudden digestive incident, or some such thing. But this idea, as soon as I had conceived it, struck me as dangerous as well as futile;

TWO—continue to put up with her horrifying stories while holding true to my nighttime resolve: to be overly polite to and hypocritical with the process-server in the preposterous hope of influencing his principles, as well as his apparently rigid feelings, and to gain, who knows, his indulgence;

THREE—slam the door in both their faces.

After diverse procrastinations, I opted for solution two. In other words, for good sense. In other words, for cowardice.

Forgive my mother's attitude, I said to the process-server in a final attempt at diplomacy, terrifically tormented as I was by the desire to appear, in every respect, conventional. My mother is finding it rather hard to endure our present tribulations. Especially as she is unwell, I emphasized, infusing my voice with an exaggerated disquiet. It's a state of nervous shock, Monsieur, linked to the death of her brother, a condition which, for reasons it would take too long to expound, resurfaced more than thirty years after the event, in 1978, to be exact.

Ever since then, I said, my mother has been continually returning to that year of 1943 which was at once the year of her brother's death, of Putain's glory, and of the reign of Bousquet-Darnand, as though her entire life, my entire life, all lives were condensed in these events, and as though her future, my future and the future of the world depended upon the meaning that she was striving to attribute to them.

The process-server, who was at present observing the pink satin bag that hung on the bathroom door beneath the post-office almanac and which was stuffed with reminder letters, unpaid bills, and leaflets announcing that week's bargain offers at the supermarket, the process-server looked up at me with an expression in which I thought I discerned a sort of astonishment. I tried therefore to make my thesis more precise. With the subtlety, conciseness, and sophistication that distinguish me, I attempted to render Mama's machinations, which could, at first sight, appear a little strange, intelligible to him.

My mother, Mr Process-Server, cannot tell past from present, day from night, nor the living from the dead. It's a highly atypical mental illness, which is immune to the most drastic of psychiatric treatments as well as Lourdes water, we've tried everything. To be more precise, I said, my mother lives simultaneously in the past and the present and their respective forms of chaos tend to become entangled and to balloon to quite apocalyptic proportions. Mama, in any case, asserts that the Apocalypse has already taken place. She proclaims this to the blind and to the deaf, whose number in this country is legion. A two-headed calf has been born in Chernobyl, she announces, it's a sure sign. We are heading for the precipice, she utters, raising her voice to an oracular pitch that gives me goose bumps. Evil is in power. Children commit murder. Everything's up for sale. In the sacred woods the shrines are now all empty. The world is in love with gold. Gold corrupts justice and warps the law. The Apocalypse, my dear, is being fulfilled before our very eyes. And while the mass of moronic humanity continue blithely to fornicate, to befuddle their minds and to kill one another with enthusiasm, the world, my dear, is on the road to ruin, and Putain, Darnand, and their zealots are present on all fronts, they triumph, my dear, they triumph. These are not the prophesies of an embittered madwoman as you might believe, since it is my misfortune that you too take me for a madwoman, but just the facts that I confine myself to stating, I cannot switch on the TV without seeing some form of carnage that they have fomented, disaster follows upon disaster, war upon war, Germany is at our gates, my God, let's flee from the wicked for it seems to me they are without number, they are everywhere.

It is in front of her TV screen, Mr Process-Server, that my mother constructs her catastrophic interpretation of the signs of disaster. As a result, I've come to think of that apparatus as the natural extension of my mother's ravings, the perfect mirror to her hallucinations. At times I find myself believing, Monsieur, that the world in which I live is nothing but a fraud, a sinister fable created out of thin air by Mama's diseased mind, which may at any moment keel over and plunge into the abyss. Taking me down with it.

I stopped short, surprised I had talked so much. I realized that, despite the repulsion I felt for this process-server, I was giving away secrets that I had never previously divulged. I felt ashamed. I didn't know what had prompted me. Was it my abject desire to procure his pity? A long suppressed need to share with some living soul the secret of my mother's follies, about which I had always remained silent in order to avoid fuelling gossip, always so vigorous in our part of the world? Or was I merely imitating those repugnant, lonely people who never miss an opportunity, whether at the hairdresser's or the grocer's, to spew out their petty inner feelings and resentments?

However it may be, I was now talking to the process-server about my mother in a way that I had never dared to do with anyone, though I did, in my confusion, perceive the inappropriateness of such an outpouring.

I'm finding it increasingly hard to put up with Mama and her abominable predictions, Monsieur, I admitted, and I feel that her madness is creeping up on me insidiously with each new day.

Do I appear mad to you, Monsieur?

Without replying, the process-server looked at me with an indecipherable expression, neither hostile nor kind, then with a firm step he strode to the couch and jotted down: a traditional two-seater couch, covered in green repp, but threadbare and ragged at its right-hand armrest . . .

ELEVEN

It was on a couch just like that that your grandmother collapsed when she returned from the café, my mother said as she lit a Gitane.

She's off on one again, I whispered furtively to the process-server, while rotating the tip of my index finger against my temple.

And that evening, my dear, your grandmother didn't go out and dig her vegetable garden like she used to every evening. She didn't address a single friendly word to . . .

Each time she looks into the depths of her past, she loses her footing, I muttered, adopting an expression of pity.

. . . to her hens which she had gone out to feed with our excrement. Neither did she cry out for joy before the peonies which were beginning to open their red hearts, nor did she give me the mambo lesson she had promised. That evening, your grandmother, my dear, without any irritation, listened to Filo describing her nightmare about food and recapitulating for the thousandth time the list of foods of which she was so hideously deprived. And all throughout the meal, your grandmother remained encased in a sort of pained indifference, her eyes fixed on the oil lamp that she had rigged up with a tin of sardines obtained at the cost of infinite negotiations from Monsieur Legoumaut. And when we lay down in the icy double bed that we had been sharing since my father had left for the war, I sensed that for a long time she just lay there with her eyes open interrogating the darkness.

Mama you talk too much, you'll tire yourself, I said, to prompt her not to go on so long.

Don't interrupt me all the time, my mother told me, moving straight on:

Your grandmother spent the week with a hunted, guilty look on her face that I'd never seen on her before, neglecting the hens, the flowers, Victoire our cat, and me, while listening distractedly to the terrible fulminations that Henriot was launching on the airwaves courtesy of wireless telegraphy and which usually sent a shiver down her spine, and suddenly she was quite indifferent to Tino Rossi's faggotty cooing on Radio Andorra which she normally listened to in a swoon, humming along to his honeyed words. Screwed down behind her sewing machine, she mechanically ran the fabric backward and forward beneath the needle, then suddenly got up, ran out into the garden and for hours stood stock-still observing the imperceptible movement of the elms, attentive to a murmuring that no one else could hear.

And on the Friday evening, my dear, when my brother Jean arrived from Toulouse where he spent the week, your grandmother announced that she was going to her sister Thérèse's place, from whom she had heard nothing in eleven years, she'd be back the day after tomorrow, so don't worry, Jean, you look after your sister, she's not to go to the river on her own, what with the current.

The following day, your grandmother caught the seven o'clock bus to the Toulouse railroad station, and there she got on a train for Vichy. For, as she explained to us many months later, your grandmother, my dear, during the week following that horrible letter, got it into her head to go and request an audience with Marshal Pétain who, every Thursday, threw open his doors to the good people of France. And throughout the journey, which to her seemed interminable, she went over in her mind a thousand times the terms in which she would address the Savior of the Fatherland.

Trembling, she would enter the Holy Ark.

She would prostrate herself at his feet, no, that was a bit excessive, rather she would perform a slight genuflection and would lower her gaze, streaming with admiration, into the blue depths of the Marshal's eyes.

Your Excellency, no, that was far too reverential, Venerated Maréchal, no, that sounded like ass-kissing. Would she instead address him as the Maréchalissimo? Your grandmother, my dear, hesitated at length between the various epithets by which the press and the radio referred to Pétain: the Supreme Chief who had snatched the Fatherland from disaster (not bad) or the Infallible Guide who had saved us from the serial murders planned by the Communists (too long), the Guardian of the West (clichéd), the good and fair Benefactor of France who, inspired by a calm sense of purpose, had eliminated individualism, a drug worse than alcohol (too tangled), the Hero who had vanquished the forces of Evil and struggled triumphantly against class struggle which was a fantasy of foreign Jews (no less tangled), the most French of Frenchmen, the Great Oak, the Providential Father of the Pacified Fatherland, the Egg of the Eagle, the Nazis' Sweetheart (no, not that), the Man Born To Lead, the Living Myth, the Victor of Verdun who longed for France to be as pure and timeless as the snows of Kilimanjaro, the Conquering Caesar who had quelled the Spanish criminals, those savages who, having slit the throats of all the priests in their own country, imagined they could come and start all over again in France, well!, they could think again, the Maréchal snickered, they're out of luck!, he said, thank you Monsieur le Maréchal for your implacable wisdom, the Ultra-Chief who watched over the purity of our race like a mother watches over her little ones (too long), the Mighty Lightning-Conductor (ridiculous), the Pharaonic Chief (too demagogical), the Illustrious Friend of the Generalissimo Francisco Franco, the Admirable Admirer of the Ascetic Salazar, Providence's Chosen Instrument of God, the Man who has sacrificed himself on the altar of the Fatherland, the Defender of France who had but one fault, that he was mortal . . .

Monsieur le Maréchal, she would say to him quite simply, in view of the honor that you bestow upon me by granting me a few minutes of your precious time, might I submit to your immense clear-sightedness some of my modest reflections? Here, Monsieur le Maréchal, is what is being plotted behind your back, and she would set out the facts without defaming the informers but by naming the defamed in order that they might be exonerated. I do not at all contest the fact, she would say to him, that the Fatherland must be defended against the plots of bloodthirsty terrorists in the pay of Bolsheviks and that the said Bolsheviks must be destroyed without pity. I can perfectly well see that, just as you argue, the agents of subversion, who are displaying ever greater cruelty and offending against the honor of France, as indeed your posters so effectively illustrate, must be denounced. It is the sacred duty of every citizen. I have besides a considerable taste for the epistolary medium (diplomacy, diplomacy, she kept repeating to herself, therein lies the key to any negotiation) and I do not question for a second the moral stature of those who denounce in writing the abominable actions of the plotters. But might one not, she would insinuate to him having completed these delicate circumlocutions, do away with the rewards offered to sycophants or at the very least reduce them in such a way as to discourage those who issue denunciations for reasons of venality? For people are people, she would add, and money hardens their vices.

Thus, in spite of the immense devotion that you inspire in me and the boundless adulation that I pledge to you, no, that I feel for you, she would say to him, might I dare suggest, Monsieur le Maréchal, that you encourage your people to contemplate the merits of others rather than snuffling through their vices?

As will be obvious, Monsieur le Maréchal, I am persuaded that the decision to reward informers cannot have originated in a superior soul such as your own. I should therefore wish, on the grounds of my filial and respectful attachment to your person, to place you on your guard against those among your entourage whose advice is deeply flawed and who, out of cowardice, keep you in ignorance of the French people, concealing from you their baseness as if it were yours, thereby preventing you from squarely facing the bitter, as they say, reality.

That's when she would strike her great blow.

Rid yourself of this herd of swine, she would tell him. Chase out this festering flock of frantically scheming flatterers who flatter to get, flatter to reach, flatter as they crap, this scum that lusts after titles and medals, this rout of rapacious roués racked with ambition, who lie themselves hoarse, this heap of incompetents and grifters, as greedy as they are base, who feed you any old fib, intent on gulling you and dulling your glory, while under its cover they thrive like lice. You will forgive me for speaking plainly, Monsieur le Maréchal, if I tell you that those people are pulling the wool over your eyes, especially Laval, she would cunningly add, repeating the lessons that Larzillière and Desmottes, who had been her mentors before becoming her enemies, had rehearsed a hundred times.

I've finished, I've finished, Monsieur le Maréchal, but it's vital that those swine depart at once, they can all go to hell, no offense to yourself intended, for it is because of them that your vision of the Fatherland is mistaken, they are constantly lying to you, plotting behind your back, planning at the very dead of night, even within your own residence, their count-less wretched conspiracies that miscarry the moment they're conceived.

You are, your grandmother would say before leaving, you are a pure man encircled by jackal. And all of these jackal must be liquidated. Jackal or jackals? Mama asked the process-server, who didn't reply.

The Marshal would thank her effusively. Thank you, Chère Madame. Madame who, in fact? Madame Jeanne Mélie, at your service. Do you have any children, Chère Madame Amélie? Two little marvels, Monsieur le Maréchal, my Jean who is eighteen years old and my Rose who is going on seven. My congratulations, Chère Madame. Thank you, Monsieur le Maréchal. And then she would leave, her heart full of joy, her soul gossamer-light, etcetera, etcetera.

On arriving at the station, your grandmother, my dear, Mama said, felt momentarily disoriented by the crowd of faces and a buzz of excitement that was quite unfamiliar to her (in all her life, she had only been into town on two occasions). She was overcome for a moment by the childish terror that she might get lost, but so great was her resolve that she managed to conquer her fear. She asked the direction to the Hôtel du Parc and set off on foot. She hurried through the streets, passing women standing in line outside empty grocers shops, saw without registering them the notices plastered on the walls proclaiming: THE BLACK MARKET IS A CRIME, PLACE YOUR TRUST IN THE GERMAN SOLDIERS, but each time she glimpsed the giant portrait of the Marshal she slowed down to draw courage from his august countenance.

On arriving in front of the Hôtel du Parc, where a crowd of passersby in gabardine coats and trilby hats was milling about, your grandmother caught sight of eight or nine state-security guards on sentry duty at the propylaeum, including four typical members of Darnand's Militia: a mean look on their faces and a finger on the trigger, about as amiable as this character here, Mama said, eyeing the process-server who didn't react, and a sentry posted in his box, rigorously perpendicular to the pavement, with a terrible air of boredom stuck to his face.

Your grandmother, my dear, was not expecting to find so many guards outside the home of the Savior of France, but she imagined that they were all there in order to hold in check the people's love for its Chief, a love which, as everybody knows, was immeasurable.

She resolved to address the guard who seemed to her to be the least surly, with her heart beating hard she approached the perpendicular sentry with the terrible air of boredom stuck to his face, pardon me Monsieur, and, bursting with emotion, she requested kind permission to report to the Benefactor of the Fatherland an ignominious action to which she had been witness and, when all is said and done, accomplice, if you please.

Move along, said the sentry and his face repetrified so immediately that your grandmother doubted whether he had spoken.

Bewildered, she took a few steps in the direction of the carbine-wielding guards whom she found somewhat unwelcoming, indeed downright unfriendly, but no sooner had she opened her mouth than a circle formed around her.

Your grandmother, my dear, then understood that the passersby in gabardine coats and trilby hats were in fact just cops. She explained to them very patiently that she had just traveled over five hundred kilometers inspired by the most holy of causes: to lift the scales from the Maréchal's eyes and to put him in the picture about . . .

Your papers, snapped a police officer, who scrutinized her photograph, made a skeptical grimace, raised his eyes to her, and made a still more skeptical grimace. And your grandmother, my dear, began to tremble with anxiety, for the photograph, taken in the year of her marriage, looked nothing like her.

Just as the cop, with apparent reluctance, was handing back her papers, a Militiaman grabbed her brutally by the arm, Clear out of here, Marshal Pétain has no time to waste with nuts.

And as your grandmother struggled one more time to explain her sublime crusade, another Militiaman, who was built like a colossus and reminded her of the stockier of the Jadre twins, shouted, Get the fuck out of here, this isn't the place for sluts, and he gave her such a shove in the back she almost fell over.

Are these the methods from which you draw your inspiration? Mama asked the process-server in a playful and almost chatty tone of voice (for Mama was a peerless expert at the good-cop bad-cop routine), while the process-server, squatting before the large cupboard, strove to make a clear list of the disparate objects heaped there haphazardly: an electric toaster that had come to pieces; a small Camping Gaz stove; six pairs of shoes with worn-out heels; a mayonnaise whisk; an alarm clock with a broken glass; a black plastic handbag; a chipped ashtray in the shape of a heart; a torn red umbrella.

And then your grandmother, who had your character, my dear, don't be angry, your grandmother flew into a rage, swore, stamped her feet and kicked all six of the police officers who had now thrown themselves upon her in an attempt to overpower her.

She was bundled into one of those old black front-wheel drive Citroëns that sped off, like in a Simenon crime novel. Heading for Hôtel Lardy. A terrifying place. A kind of hell. It was just a matter of dealing with some minor formalities, the cops said. You will have recognized this, my dear, as what is known as a euphemism, which is a poetical procedure much used by these new-type rhetoricians.

At that very moment . . .

TWELVE

At that very moment, Marshal Pétain was receiving at his table, in the dining room of the Hôtel du Parc, Doctor Ménétrel, who at one and the same time served him as factotum, devoted doctor, sworn courtier, faithful flatterer, his smug bastard son, his personal anti-Semite, infamous propagandist, and the only living soul, other than Pétain's wife, Madame la Maréchale herself, who might on certain occasions address him as Philippe, perhaps one day he would even make so bold as to call him simply Phil, or Phiphi, and the only person who dared stand up to him on serious matters, especially on the matter of the Jews on which the Marshal did sometimes demonstrate, you must forgive me, Monsieur le Maréchal, an overly kind nature, obviously I am not speaking of your friendship with the Marquise de Chasseloup-Laubat, that's your private life, but your excessive indulgence toward people of that particular race could be mistaken, I take the liberty of warning you, for a sign of weakness, do not misunderstand me, Monsieur le Maréchal, it is not that I am criticizing your . . .

Bernard Ménétrel endeavored to invite each day to the Marshal's dinner table two or three handpicked important people whose job it was to keep repeating to the Marshal that he was the Venerated Leader of the French and the Savior of the Fatherland who was ensuring that righteousness triumphed, for the Marshal never tired of hearing himself being praised to the heavens, but asked for more and more. Who was it who wrote, Mama questioned me, that to know a person thoroughly you should observe how they accept praise? Pliny the Younger, I said. Correct, Mama said.

So that day the Marshal was flanked by: l'Abbé Bouillon, Chaplain to the Militia, quivering with confusion, blushing and gushing, hanging from the lips of the great man as if sipping from the chalice, simpering in admiration and constantly making silly faces, applauding everything and assenting to everything, even to the Marshal's silences; and by Monsieur the Director of Technical Monitoring, who had been summoned expressly to demonstrate to the Marshal, with supporting evidence, the veneration that the French people felt toward his venerable person, for this veneration had been measured scientifically, I must emphasize sci-en-ti-fi-cal-ly by my technical staff, here are the numbers, which speak volumes: of the 2,336,456 letters opened in a single month and the 921,532 telephone conversations tapped, we have counted 3,257,906 expressions of confidence and faith in the Marshal, fifty-six of sympathy and only eighteen of hostility. How many? asked the Marshal, who was hard of hearing. Eight, the Director of Technical Monitoring muttered feebly, glancing uncertainly at Ménétrel. There do of course remain some imponderables. Unless Monsieur le Maréchal prefers to deem the imponderables null and void. Which would, of course, be an excellent solution.

The Marshal, with an affable but imperious gesture, summoned the butler, who came running, his face ecstatic. The venerated Marshal wanted a second helping of *petits pois à la française*, it was his favorite dish. Madame la Maréchale signaled her disagreement by giving Dr Ménétrel a stony stare. Pétain's wife, whose first name was Virginie, took the view that the Marshal ate too much. Dr Ménétrel, attentive and maternal, poured a trickle of water into the Savior of France's glass, already three quarters full with Château-Lafite 1934, and Madame la Maréchale blinked her consent, dear Ménétrel!

While the venerated Marshal was making a pig of himself, your grandmother, who had been conveyed, as I have said, to Hôtel Lardy, was demanding a face-to-face meeting with the Principal Inspector, setting off an explosion of hilarity among the police officers. You're out of your mind! one of them said to her finally, once they had all calmed down.

For dessert, Madame la Maréchale decided on a *tarte à l'orange* which she did her utmost to chew in tiny mouthfuls in order to attenuate the disastrous effect that her large lipless mouth exerted on her husband's guests. At that time, we should recall, the fashion was for women to have small orifices.

The Benefactor of France, he who had saved the honor of the country from being worm-eaten by anarchy and socialism, stuffed himself with strawberries topped with Chantilly cream and ordered a coffee laced with cognac. It was at such moments, between the dessert and the coffee laced with cognac, that the Marshal would become amiable. With droplets of coffee quivering on his moustache, the Marshal would then dictate to Dr Ménétrel the decrees born of his benevolence. We, Philippe Pétain, Head of the French State, have decided that, from this day:

The women of France will no longer have to work themselves into the ground in a job that is unworthy of them and instead may stay tucked up nice and warm in their darling little homes waiting patiently for their prisoner-husbands to return from their "camping trip." How generous, how munificent that is!

Our champion athlete, Jean Borotra, will be in charge of a number of work sites where young people from all backgrounds will be able to take part in patriotic activities such as cutting down trees and paving roads, sit around a camp fire singing *Maréchal nous voilà*, and wash their bodies in cold water, all of which activities represent, quite apart from their undeniable patriotic virtues, an excellent corrective to libidinous urges, two birds with one stone. What an excellent idea!

The Jews will no longer need to trouble themselves with running their businesses, others will do that in their place. What forbearance! And how charitable!

Marshal Pétain was now tired of being amiable. He fell silent. His eyelids were heavy and sleepiness welled up within him, starting from his feet.

Monsieur Lafreu, in charge of the Industrial Amenities Plan, was hurriedly summoned to prevent the Marshal from dozing off. Lafreu was the emotional type. He stuttered, spluttered, begged forgiveness, blushed, plunged into yet deeper confusion, and then set out, in a strangled voice, his scheme for sixteen soads—begging your pardon, for sixteen roads all converging like the spokes of a wheel on Paris, leading to sixteen enormous monumental grates—begging your pardon—gates to be known as the Marshal's Gates, an awe-inspiring project for a personality who is no less, slight cough, awe-inspiring.

But the Marshal was nobody's fool. He would be dead and buried by the time the roads were completed, so he wasn't going to bother listening to the rest. His chin slumped on his flaccid old man's neck, his mouth fell open and he sank into satiated sleep.

At that very moment, my dear, your grandmother was being led into a room stinking of disinfectant that contained

84

nothing but a table and a grayish wooden bench against the wall.

Two hours later, a police officer stormed into the room, a little like the way in which this character did, Mama said, jabbing her chin toward the process-server who was still squatting in front of the large cupboard, busily sifting through our junk. He's making one hell of a mess, she then loudly exclaimed, ignoring my desperate signals to her to keep her voice down.

The police officer, my dear, threw himself on your grandmother, who was terrified, foraged frantically in her pockets, emptied out her purse with the exasperation of a psychopath and, in a paroxysm of tics and spasms, scattered on the table her papers, her bright red lipstick, the photograph of Jean and me beneath the elm trees, her broaches and baubles, her horn comb, her crocheted purse and a letter folded in four onto which your grandmother slapped her hand.

Following his nap, the Venerated Marshal shut himself up in his overheated study at the Pavillon Sévigné in the company of his faithful Ménétrel who read him his correspondence, sorted into three categories: one, personal letters; two, letters of denunciation; three, official letters.

Ménétrel began with the first pile and opened four of the three thousand that arrived each day comparing the Marshal to Jesus, to Saint Louis, to the Pope, to Chevalier Bayard, and to all that is greatest and most beautiful on earth, and the Marshal blinked because he was moved, each time the Marshal was moved he blinked, and the more the Marshal was moved the more he blinked, it was a great joy for all the French to see their blinking Marshal, and all his nearest spent their time anxiously monitoring the speed of his blinks, the top speed ever achieved being six blinks per second. *Oh France! Oh*

Mother Sweet! Oh Fatherland Fine! / Fervently bent o'er your broken wing, / With grieving soul do I divine / Thy ravaged countenance and wounded limb. All right, all right, snapped the Marshal, who detested poetry.

Ménétrel read another two or three extracts, finishing as was his habit with a couple of smutty letters to which the Marshal, his eyelids flickering, listened enraptured, why is it that old men are so lecherous? Mama wondered. I fuck your venerated Marshal's prick, Ménétrel read out, and I suck it with veneration, my venerated Marshal, and I take it and . . . It appears to be proven, Mama said, that a great majority of women are sexually attracted by dominant types since they imagine them to be dominant as much in the act of fornication as in the general affairs of life, at least when they're not being merely infantile, sniveling and sickeningly sentimental. From which it follows, Mama said, that the majority of women are imbeciles. I regret to state this fact. Have you, Professor, observed this as I have? The process-server, his nose buried in our cupboard, did not deign to make his opinion known.

Ménétrel began on the second pile: the letters of denunciation. The Marshal did not enjoy these, but he was Head of State and therefore could not turn a blind eye to the secrets that the French people concealed in the dark recesses of their hearts. Venerque, Haute-Garonne, January 12, 1943, Most Venerated Marshal, We have the honor of drawing your attention to the case of Robert Biron, inhabitant of Venerque, supposedly suffering from rheumatism, who has been scandalously deemed unfit for compulsory labor service though in fact he possesses a powerful physique and an . . . Pass it on to Bousquet, it's his job.

At the end of the afternoon, your grandmother was pushed into Comissioner Henry's office, Are you going to tell me what the fuck you've come here for, are you going to tell me, for Christ's sake? the fearsome Commissary roared. Your grandmother, my dear, didn't dare answer back. Besides, in her terror, she didn't know what to mention and what to keep quiet about. Are you going to spit it out, for Christ's sake? Commissary Henry shouted, banging his fist on the desk. And as my mother, terrified, said nothing, he leapt up and grabbed her by the chin, What were you fucking playing at outside the Hôtel du Parc? Are you going to tell me, for Christ's sake? All right. Madame is putting on airs, Madame wants to keep her little secrets to herself, Madame thinks maybe I'm going to wait all night for her to open her mouth? Strip her! he yelled out to the police officers. A total body search! Total, I said! You want me to draw you a picture?

On the stroke of four o'clock, the Savior of France commenced his short post-prandial stroll, taking strides seventy-five centimeters in length, an incontestable sign of inner harmony, flanked by Ménétrel and four plain-clothes policemen. The outdoor air perked him up and he began at once to quaver out the prohibitions to be enacted in his forthcoming decrees:

Bernard, please take a note:

First, I prohibit the wastage of bread.

What a remarkable decision, Monsieur le Maréchal!

Second, I prohibit the use of epithets.

That's admirable, Monsieur le Maréchal, how bold!

Thirdly, I prohibit dance halls, hotbeds of antipatriotism and scarcely compatible with the dignity of France such as I understand it. In Ménétrel's ear, Don't you think that the foxtrot, that dance imported directly from England and which consists in one disjointed and lascivious step forward, then one back, then one to the side, then again one forward, then back, then to the side, and so on, don't you think that the fox-trot is in fact a vertical version of . . .

Disgusting! Dr Ménétrel exclaimed.

As he passed by, an elegantly attired lady opened a stupid mouth and placed a hand on her heart, the very portrait of veneration. Let us note that the said two movements were executed synchronously.

At that precise moment, your grandmother was being ordered to take off her clothes, and to be quick about it. Dying of shame, your grandmother undressed and with one frantic hand held out her clothes to the policeman while the other covered her pubis. This modest little movement tipped the policeman (already highly agitated) right over the edge so that he began first to tap at the hems of her clothing with quick little jabs, and then to sink his raging pocket knife into the epaulettes of her overcoat, which, however, disgorged its stuffing and nothing else, then finally he stalked off convulsively to pastures new.

At the end of the afternoon, the Marshal presented a fran-cisque badge to a bellhop who nearly fainted, and then shut himself up in his chamber and challenged his wife to a little game of bezique, at which he could not refrain from cheating. His wife cried out, Cheat, I saw you! but the Marshal exclaimed, It's not true, you're lying! so Madame resigned herself, with a sigh, to allowing her husband to win. They had to avoid at all cost the kind of old people's argument that crashes through a hotel's walls and pierces the ears of ministers close by, who would be listening intently, day and night.

Then, with that eager but repellent expression so characteristic of old people faced with the things they crave, the Marshal remained for a long moment, his glutton's eyes glued on the photographs of his people.

For the people loved their Maréchal.

And the Maréchal loved the fact that the people loved him.

For the Maréchal loved himself.

The aged autophiliac would wallow for hours in the contemplation of images of his glory captured during his numerous tours: wild crowds, mayors bellowing hysterically from garlanded balconies, cheap promises thrown to the imbecilic mob, the hurrahs! the clamor, the delirious leader-worship, Praise be to our Maréchal, God protect our Maréchal, Eternal Glory to our Maréchal, the unending ovations that went straight to his heart and brought tears to his eyes, all this emotion is going to kill him, feared his wife, Not at all, quite the opposite, said Dr Ménétrel reassuringly, empty phrases garnished with sublime words, the Fatherland, the Fatherland, the Fatherland, the Fatherland, the Fatherland, the Fatherland, the Fatherland, the fanfares, the pomp, the trumpets, the panegyrics by the shovelful, the earnest speeches enjoining the nation's youth to go work like slaves for free in the Building Yards of France, *Allons enfants de la Patri-euh-euh*, Masses in memory of the thousands who had croaked, glory be to those that croaked, the photographers clustered in swarms endlessly taking steps backward, forward and sideways, like a foxtrot, the young girls in uniforms throwing pink roses in his path, I feel faint, the nuns overcome by an orgasm of mysticism, such things can indeed happen, crossing themselves whenever he appeared in a vision to them, the enthralled mothers stretching out their quivering hands in the hope of touching, what?

the hem of his overcoat! the schoolchildren chanting as they pledged their oaths to serve him and follow his footsteps, all the ambience of a historical epic.

At six o'clock, two policemen from Venerque appeared at the house where my brother and I, beside ourselves with anxiety, were awaiting our mother's return, Police! Open Up! saying they were empowered by the authorities of Vichy, ripping open the wardrobes, smashing the cupboards, ransacking the chests of drawers, turning over the mattresses, what were they looking for? they didn't know, their superior as always had been vague, but the law was the law and orders were orders, lifting the carpets, upturning the garbage can, emptying the bag of cinders, emptying the boxes of sprouting potatoes, emptying everything that could be emptied, like this boor who's really beginning to piss me off, my mother grumbled, fixing her eyes on the back of the process-server who had been exhuming our junk for hours now.

At 7.30: Marshal Pétain went to do a poo.

At 7.40: he admired his presents.

Because presents simply flooded into his home. Why is it, Mama broke off, that presents always go to those who are already up to their necks in them? Presents arrived from every corner of France, cross-stitched embroidery depicting the Marshal in every imaginable position, vases, medals, jewels by the thousands, If I listened to my own feelings, his wife mumbled, I'd chuck the whole lot in the garbage, caskets incrusted with seashells spelling out his name, doilies embroidered with the initials PP entwined: they had horrors to burn. Or to sell.

What if we sold them? suggested Madame la Maréchale, a very sensible person. No question of it! The Marshal was against it. He couldn't possibly part with a single object, not even a tie pin. An anal sadist, that's what he was. It's obvious you're not the one who does the cleaning up round here! his wife chided him.

But the Marshal never loosened his grip on the reins of authority. Never. Even in his private life, Monsieur le Maréchal remained the uncontested and omniscient leader, and the horrible presents kept piling up on the tables, the chests of drawers and all over the floor. What a mess, his wife complained, for the apartment of a Head of State!

At eight o'clock, the overexcited policeman ordered your grandmother to put her clothes back on. Then he ordered her to follow him into another room. Then he ordered her to sit on a bench. Then he ordered her not to approach the stove. Then he ordered himself to stand at attention outside the door. Then a few seconds later, he ordered himself to fall out, out you fall, and he obeyed himself immediately.

At nine o'clock, the Marshal, comfortably tucked up in his fine brass bed, opened *Gaspard in the Mountains* and fell asleep at the second page.

You can keep right on searching, you won't find a thing! Not a goddamned thing! my mother yelled at the process-server as if suddenly reminded of his presence. The process-server looked at her without any expression, with at most a slight quivering of his left eyebrow.

Your grandmother, my dear, my mother resumed, as she flopped onto a chair, your grandmother remained two whole days shivering on her bench without drinking or eating, and she had every opportunity to examine a hundred times the Legion-des-Volontaires-Français posters plastered all over the walls and which invited young people to die for their grateful Fatherland, for to die for one's grateful Fatherland was, in those days, Mother said, an honor, dying for one's Fatherland was a bit like getting promoted, rising through the ranks of death.

One of the said posters portrayed a soldier with a jutting jaw, standing in a flattering pose, with a stubborn look and the squared chin of someone who knows what he wants, triumphs over everything, and marches straight on into a future governed by the eagle of dementia itself, which in its turn is topped by a leader railing against those foreign crooks, do you follow me? and this soldier reminded your grandmother of the stockier of the Jadre twins. Whereupon she felt the longing to embrace us, Jean and me, in her arms, to call us my chicks, my little ones, my mouth-watering beauties, my angels fallen from the sky, till the Jadre twins no longer frightened us, and she burst out sobbing murmuring through her tears, My chicks, my darlings, my beloved hearts, my wild treasures.

But, as she told us much later, this spell in prison, however trying, turned out to be very instructive for her, since it accomplished in two days what might have taken a whole year or even longer. In this brief moment, she felt, she said, her mental faculties attain a point of extreme incandescence. She experienced a kind of illumination, though a dark illumination, one ought to say a fire, that threw a violent light on things while at the same time darkening them, and that showed her the Earth covered with a dirty, somber and frightening veil. It was, she said, as if the world and its very spirit had been turned inside out, laying bare their inner nature, contaminated, purulent, and black with blood.

But this transformation, however radical, only manifested itself in her gradually. Your grandmother, my dear, began by making caustic little remarks in the café, little witticisms about Putain, then bit by bit her anger rose, and rose, and . . .

. . . and one dark day in January, at the tobacco dealer's who sold:

Pétain busts complete with stripes, stars, sashes, ribbons, braid, and lace, making him look exactly like a general in a comic opera, don't say that!

portraits of Pétain, left-profile, bare-headed,

portraits of Pétain, three-quarter profile,

portraits of Pétain, right-profile, wearing a hat, expression cold and severe (coldness and severity, it's a well-known fact, impress the populace),

giant portraits of Pétain fighting off drowsiness, both hands laid flat on his desk, his chest swollen with sacred love of the Fatherland (very highly prized),

portraits of Pétain dressed up as a station master, his uniform so stiff it seems to be holding him upright,

portraits of Pétain on a garden bench, *sic transit gloria mundi*,

portraits of Pétain standing, marble-faced, his turquoise-blue gaze reflecting his lofty soul intent on its mission, matching kitsch tunic, format 19x26cm, on cardboard, twelve francs each, five for fifty,

marshal's batons (I have often wondered what purpose this type of baton might serve: a democratic version of the royal scepter? an implement for beating recalcitrant ministers?

or a phalloid ornament proportional in size to the prestige of
its proprietor?),

portraits of Pétain in full uniform (uniforms, as is well
known, excite the admiration of paupers and imbeciles), his
stony appearance, his gaze fixed on the future, the photogra-
pher concealed beneath a black sheet having just asked him to
smoothe his moustache and to focus on the windowsill, don't
move, I'll count to three,

portraits of Pétain kissing a terrified little girl (why do
the powerful have this mania for kissing children? It's highly
suspect),

portraits of Pétain in plain clothes, good-natured, conversing with the meek (one can recognize the meek by the way
they look at their feet),

portraits of Pétain stroking a lamb (a favorite among children between five and eight years of age),

portraits of Pétain thanking a peasant farmer who looks
like he has stepped straight out of a Soviet painting,

portraits of Pétain kissing the flag of the 33rd infantry
regiment,

five-franc calendars with twelve detachable photographs
of Pétain,

plaster statuettes of Pétain, three finishes available, bronze,
ivory, or earthen,

postcards bearing a picture portrait of Pétain

ashtrays bearing a picture portrait of Pétain

Pétain knife-fork-and-spoon sets

Pétain pen-and-pencil sets

Pétain propelling pencils

Pétain cigarette lighters

Pétain cigarette holders

Pétain postage stamps
Pétain handkerchiefs
Pétain pocket diaries
Pétain thermometers
Pétain escutcheons
Pétain pennants
Pétain earrings
Pétain tiepins
Pétain pipes

the whole lot piled up in a jumble on trestle tables, and
your grandmother walked up and stood right in front of the
giant two-meter by one-meter-twenty portrait of Marshal Pétain
which hung over the till and shouted Heil Putain! while doing
the Hitler salute, and Monsieur Chauchard, who had entered
the shop with his son in order to buy some stamps, looked at
her, scandalized, as if she had just dropped her panties, right
there and then, before his very eyes.

This was the start of her downfall. Or of her assumption.
No one will ever know.

For her, the tide was clearly turning.

People talked.

They claimed, Your Honor, said my mother to the process-
server, who was now measuring the dining-room table, that
her hair color was not natural, that she wore skintight trousers
with obviously lecherous intentions, and garish cherry-shaped
earrings, it looks pretty bad for a mother-of-two, that she used
tincture of iodine to draw a line up the backs of her calves
to make it look like she was wearing stockings, the whore,
that she had performed an abortion on that Spanish woman
who had then almost died, if that ever became known it was
the death penalty, that she listened to Radio Ca-ca, Radio

what? Gaga-gaulle's radio broadcast from London, and more especially the filthy harangues of a certain Schuman, with a name like that he could only be English! that she preferred, poor thing, the music of Johnny Hess or of Jerry Mengo to Gounod's *Ave Maria*, that she spared not a thought for her poor husband who was rotting in some stalag, that was perfectly true, that she didn't send her little girl to the catechism lessons given by the village priest, who liked to compare the Marshal to Jesus Christ himself and who had displayed on the wall of the presbytery the following prayer, framed by a floral frieze: *Monsieur le Maréchal, Father of the Fatherland, Give us this day our daily bread, And let us not succumb to the temptations of hunger, But deliver us instead from this evil as you have delivered us from war, The first time by victory, this time by armistice, Amen*, that she had been caught drawing a big V for victory on the pharmacist's door in bright red lipstick, quite true said Mama, that she was raising her children on modernist ideas inspired by this schoolteacher Baysse, permitting them for example to put their elbows on the table both literally and figuratively and other similar improprieties, it's a disgrace, that she's heading for trouble, that it would all end badly, very badly, I'm telling you.

Little by little, Your Honor, the talking grew louder, the gossips were unleashed, and the most extravagant of rumors circulated about my mother, that she was in the habit of singing the Pétainist anthem *Maréchal nous voilà!* with her fist raised like an anarchist, which was blasphemy, that she had magnetic powers over persons of the male sex, the slut, that she prostituted herself and gave the most fabulous blow-jobs, may I die if I lie, said Desmottes, obsessed as he was with her adorable and oh-so-shapely ass which appeared to him to be made of some kind of plastic material, he was the expert, that she exchanged torrid and bewitching correspondence with a terrorist of materialist convictions by the name of Baysse, him again, it was completely true, Mama said, besides I thought for a long time that I was his natural daughter, that she had declared to Mademoiselle Piche, who was afflicted by a concave bosom but who proved, if one scrutinized her closely enough, to belong to the female sex, that she had declared, just listen to this, that the pox and exaggerated love for the Fatherland were the two scourges of France, and that whereas there was some hope that the former might one day be susceptible to treatment, the latter remained quite incurable, since sexual perversions, she commented, are known to respond, alas, to no medicine, that while waiting in line at the cinema she had raised her voice to advise everyone to hold on to their entrance tickets because they could come in handy for wrapping up their measly meat rations, then that she had burst out laughing, what nerve, laughing at wretchedness! that she had refused to give a single cent to the children collecting money to send the prisoners a portable chapel kit including a chalice, a paten, an altar stone, a chasuble, an alb, a crucifix, a ciborium, some cruets, holy oils, some communion wine, and forty missals, and that she had objected, It would be better to send them some sausage meat, holy wafers don't exactly fill you up! that she read seditious newspapers that circulated clandestinely and one of which was called *Libération* (what an outrage!) that she had been seen posting bills bearing the words VIVE DE GAULLE, and she would pay for that.

My mother, like all generous people, could not for a single moment imagine, Your Honor, that anyone might blame her or wish her harm. That was her mistake. With all the fervor of the pure of heart, she continued to proclaim her outrageous opinions at the top of her voice, for she wished to open the eyes of all those who, like her, had been misled for so long. She continued to inveigh against Putain and his clique of scoundrels, accusing the Marshal of starving the nation, calling him a traitor and other unappealing epithets (most of which pertained to zoology), imagining naively that she was met with general approval, insulting the leader of the nation, how many years is that going to fetch? She continued to call Putain by his initials: Pee-Pee or even the old dodder, the ancient fuckhead, the old bastard, according to her moods and the atmospheric currents to which her soul was sensitive, or quite simply that old cunt.

She continued to refer to the Hôtel du Parc as the old people's home and to proclaim that as for Putain's portrait, she used it to wipe her . . . that's worth internment in the Récébédou concentration camp, such raving insanity! that as for his baton, she stuck it up her . . . and here she used her fingers to execute an infinitely graceful gesture aimed right at the middle of her rear-end . . . but that's an outrage against public decency, no more no less! that at Montoire Putain had met Hitler who had come to pay him a courtesy visit and that, by way of a gift, he had presented Hitler with a plaything, France, not bad, and some leftovers, the French. She said that? Lord Jesus! She would live to regret it!

My mother wondered aloud, and in a mocking tone of voice, whether Putain shat in his pants, whether he pissed in his uniform, whether Madame la Maréchale, yes or no, swaddled him in diapers, insulting the Head of State, that was between five and fifteen years in jail, at least, did the Marshal stink of piss? she wondered out loud, was he completely senile or was he just pretending so people would leave him in peace? mightn't he in fact be a stuffed animal? This notion struck her, in any case, as politically smart, since in her view the entire function of the Head of State was merely to play to the gallery. Besides, it's an idea I share, Mama said. And what do you think of it? she said to the process-server who was busy writing in his notebook: a dining-room table, farmhouse style, imitation oak, measuring 1.20 x 0.80 meters, good general condition.

These and similar opinions, my mother said without waiting for the process-server's reply, brought her nothing but quarrels and hostility. Most Venerquois even stopped saying hello to her. Her neighbors pleaded pressure of work to curtail their former chattering and their hellos-and-goodbyes. The village pharmacist, the instant he saw her, would become absorbed in the contemplation of his two-tone shoes, while the village priest would launch into a meditation on the grace of God that protected him from the lust of the eyes. Monsieur Legoumaut, the grocer, served her grudgingly, with the mute approval of his lady customers who surveyed her with knowing looks. The butcher swindled her openly over the weight of cutlets, but she didn't feel she had any right to protest. The notary's wife no longer brought her suits to her to tailor, neither did the wife of the hardware dealer nor the wife of the hairdresser. No one in Venerque wanted to compromise themselves by keeping such poisonous company.

Yet in her recklessness, Your Honor, she went on repeating that the Maréchal was going to take it up the . . . and laughing and pouring scorn and laying it on ever thicker, that he was finished, that he was unstable, may his soul rest in peace, that the Allies, who had just landed, were going to give him a proper beating, and she laughed at the top of her lungs.

The village authorities, quick to take offense, finally intervened and followed all her comings and goings and indeed placed the very least of her movements under strict surveillance. Evidence, insinuations, petitions, denunciations, and other forms of vomit specific to human beings, all demanding that the Offender be brought into line, poured down like rain on the desk of the village mayor. Mama's invectives against the Maréchal were polluting the atmosphere, and the impudent way she wiggled her ass, no, no, no, all well-meaning decent souls were unanimous in their agreement on at least this point. It was vital to react, in the name of public decency if nothing else. Public decency, the expression was a success, an enormous success.

They waited for my mother to commit some serious outrage or assault so they could call her to account and punish her. But as that failed to happen, the Jadre twins were allowed to do whatever they saw fit. They'd take care of her ideas, and her rear-end too.

Mama broke off to go and drink a glass of water, for the large doses of neuroleptics that she took gave her a dry mouth. Then, as if the low temperature of the water had jolted her from her dreams, Haven't you left yet? she snapped at the process-server, suddenly remembering what he was there for.

FOURTEEN

I'm in no mood to joke, the process-server replied, stung by her words.

That's what your mistake is, Mama said, a joke would be most beneficial for a mind that like yours has all the sensitivity of a stone.

For the first time since he'd arrived at our door, the process-server almost lost his sangfroid. His features contracted. His left eyebrow was lifted by a slight trembling. And several drops of perspiration pearled his forehead. He removed his spectacles. Pink little moon-shaped marks appeared on either side of his nose as though his spectacles had been ripped from his flesh. Then he took from his pocket an immaculate white handkerchief, wiped his forehead with it, returned it to his pocket and, having completed this procedure, gave me a look in which I thought I read some hint of indecision.

I responded with an expression of consternation.

I would have liked to vanish. Or to have eliminated my mother once and for all. For a moment I toyed with the unrealistic idea of injecting her with a dose of heroin, while at the same time and with great speed I contemplated ways of getting rich quick. Apart from prostitution, which was, I have to admit, very appealing, or a national lottery jackpot, which was highly improbable, nothing much came to mind. Writing? I was terribly lacking in talent. Politics? But, as Quintus Cicero so rightly insists in his *Little Election-Campaign*

Manual, one needed money for bribes, and where would I get that from?

Get out of here you bastard, my mother shouted at the process-server as she pulled the cigarette butt from her lips and flung it to the ground.

I suspected that Mama was behaving in this odious fashion for the sole purpose of exacting revenge for the tortures which she claimed I constantly inflicted upon her: the thrice-daily compulsory consumption of medications, the ban on her leaving the flat, not to mention the taunts, insults and other acts of malice fuelled by the grudge that from an early age I had harbored toward her for having dumped me so many times in foster homes (in my defense I should state that more often than not I did no more than allude to this memory), tortures, I was saying, which she took a bitter pleasure in enumerating, knowing that the very mention of them, far from flattering my vanity as it should have done, drained my morale.

Or perhaps my mother believed me to be in league with the process-server? That was possible. Crazy as she was. Besides, Mama spent her entire life sniffing out conspiracies the enormity of which varied from one day to the next according to the sensitivity of the radar equipment with which, she claimed, her soul was equipped, sufficiently powerful to detect her enemies in the most unlikely of hiding places, under her bed, for example, clever to think of looking there!

I told you to get out, Mama shouted at the process-server.

The least I could do was reassure him. Don't listen to my mother, Mr Process-Server, she's insane. First she mistook you for a judge and now all of a sudden she thinks you're a member of the Militia. She's talking utter nonsense, I said, slipping a hint of disdain into my voice.

Given that the supply of patience I had so far deployed had had no effect whatsoever, I was now determined, however regretfully, to alter my stance, as it were, and train my shotgun on my mother. For since it was vital, as I believed, to reach some accommodation with this process-server, I might as well work on it before the situation degenerated. I opted therefore to make my allegiance, in a good cause, with the enemy and officially to dissociate myself from my mother. In short, I decided to apply exactly the principles advocated by Antisthenes.

Maybe you might like to take a moment's rest, Mr Process-Server? I asked in a burst of amiability.

If you have brought along your torturer colleagues, tell them to show their faces, you bastard, my mother bellowed in a voice trembling with both sorrow and rage. My mother's coarseness was overstepping the limits. For her to react sharply to the process-server's intrusion, that was one thing. But to speak to him in such a way was really unconscionable. I was going to have to intervene. And find the right words. If there were any.

None came. I wanted to let out a savage scream, a scream to petrify the entire housing project. I stopped myself in time. But I was not able to temper the anger that was boiling in my veins.

I've had enough, more than enough, of your nonsense, I yelled. Get past it, turn the page, for Christ's sake! (The coarseness of my nature, which I had disowned and brutally suppressed, was quickly resurfacing, as was inevitable.)

How do you expect me to turn the page, as you put it, Mama replied, when the page hasn't yet been written?

Are you going to shut it? Fuck and ass! I shouted. These, my own raw words, were the only ones that came out of me

now, crude words, obscene words. Can't you see you're landing us in the shit?

We're already in the shit, replied my mother with her
unshakeable madwoman's logic.

I immediately regretted the foul language I had used. It
made me appear vulgar and implied that the feelings I bore
my mother might not be the required filial ones in which I
had hitherto unjustifiably wrapped myself. To palliate the
deplorable effects produced by my coarseness (which in fact
represented my normal language, my everyday turns of phrase
being intimately linked with the impulses of my heart, despite
my constant efforts to civilize myself and to sunder them), I
said to the process-server:

Please, sir, don't let yourself be distracted from your task
(I could hardly go wrong there), please proceed with your
work as you see fit.

And I had the feeling that he was delighted I had called
him *sir*, for ever since his arrival at our home his process-
server's authority had suffered a whole series of insults. No
doubt, I conjectured, he was inured to being insulted. Perhaps
he even did this job for the sole purpose of receiving each day
his ration of insults. That was possible, given the particular
strangeness of process-servers and the general genius of men
for ceaselessly inventing new vices and new tribulations.

Regaining his composure, the process-server jotted down in
his notebook: a pedal-powered sewing machine, brand: Singer,
model: old, stand: oak, two drawers, working order . . .

Get out of here, you bastard, my mother screamed as she
bore down on him.

Mama, if you don't stop at once, I threatened her, nearly
out of my mind, I'm phoning Dr Logos, you've been warned. I

was only trying to scare her. I knew perfectly well that neither Dr Logos nor anybody else was capable of stopping Mama once she had got going. Unless one was to consider murder, which doctors ordinarily reject. Once she was off, there was no way of stopping her, none at all. As for throwing a wrench in her works, that would be pure madness, you'd get your fingers ripped off.

How many times do I have to tell you to get the hell out of here? my mother shouted as she advanced on the process-server. *Raus*! she shouted, as she pointed him to the door. *Raus*! *Raus*! This Nazi is pissing me off, she whispered to me as an aside. And as if that were not enough, Do you want me to kick your ass? she screamed in his face.

The process-server stepped back, bumping into the table. Mama laughed wildly. I don't know what stopped me from slapping her. My patience was at an end. Stop, stop, I kept telling myself. Stop, stop, stop. But I didn't know how to put an end to the furious torrent leading us relentlessly toward some kind of dramatic dénouement. And I just hate drama. Except in romantic novels, where it's indispensable. So, deep down, I too began to scream, Get out of here, Process-Server, get out or I swear I'll do something I'll live to regret. But my lips wouldn't open. Not a sound came from my mouth. I hadn't the good fortune to be crazy like my mother and to scream at the slightest provocation. And every now and then, I'm being perfectly serious, I regretted that.

If you continue, I'm calling Dr Logos at once, was all I managed to say.

One of *your* colleagues! my mother snarled at the process-server, her face contorted with disdain.

I furtively signaled to the process-server to pay no attention to my mother's nonsense.

Nobody, my mother now whispered as if talking to herself, nobody will ever be able to convince me that Dr Logos is not a member of Darnand's Militia. I'd wager anything. Because, you know, there aren't only gangsters in the Militia, not at all. There are some very upstanding people in the Militia. Fine, large-hearted ladies, Catholic and Apostolic, young high-society girls, lacking neither ideals nor rear-ends, weeping widows in search of sexual masochism, one woe to chase away another, corpulent checkout clerks (the embodiment of honesty), tremendous writers, a whole procession of them, as well as statesmen, lawmen, henchmen, straw men, men of little worth, men of the cloth who, in the combined name of Christ and Darnand, a pair of colleagues that is, who practice with fanatical zeal the love of humankind, given that they don't have much opportunity to practice love *tout court*, and an entire contingent, I almost forgot, of avaricious and hateful old maids who give alms to the poor, sorry, to the meek, handing out their old castoffs and leftovers.

I'm quite positive, Mama said, that Dr Logos secretly works for the Militia. I'd bet my life on it. And besides, whenever I confess my suspicions to him, Dr Logos is very careful not to deny them, he says neither yes nor no, he says hmm hmm while jotting down his notes, hmm, hmm, for Dr Logos says hmm hmm to everything, I'm going to marry Alain Delon and run away with him to a Caribbean paradise, hmm hmm, or go on a cruise on the Nile with either Bill Gates or Antonio Banderas, I can't make my mind up, hmm hmm, and what if I beat your face to a pulp, you asshole, hmm hmm, always hmm hmm, that's all he can say, and what if I killed you! I burst out laughing and Dr Logos jots down in his file, with frightening seriousness: *unmotivated laughter accompanied by aggressive interjections revealing a psychotic personality structure.*

However much Dr Logos puts on his unctuous priest's voice, his unctuous priest's manners and his air of calculated kindness, no one in the world will ever convince me that he doesn't belong to the Militia and that he isn't utterly resolved to neutralize me. For he trembles to hear me proclaiming the heretofore well-hidden horror stories about Putain and the other swine, all the paralipomena, my dear, that I am quite alone in denouncing (there she went again). For Dr Logos, Mama said, delicate soul that he is, and highly refined too, Dr Logos is so constituted that he doesn't hate those who commit evil half as much as those who name it. His is not a unique case, it seems. Rumor has it that this syndrome is extremely widespread among our compatriots. It's so tiresome. But, however common it may be, Dr Logos's behavior is no less stupid. Some day or another everything will come out, Mama exalted, you can't prevent a volcano erupting and bearing all before it, it's totally idiotic to try. And if he believes, this imbecile, that fifty drops of Haldol morning, noon, and night are going to keep me quiet, he's making a mistake.

What's more, Mama said, Dr Logos is completely incapable of uttering a single word of consolation. For a doctor, my dear, you must admit that's some defect. Never a pat on the shoulder. Never a smile. Never any sign of kindness. Nothing.

Why does one have to submit to beings whose souls are less generous than our own? Mama complained. It's dreadful. But I'm not frightened of Dr Logos, she said, getting to her feet. However much he assails me with his neuroleptics and however securely he locks me into his diagnostic pigeonholes, however often he labels me a madwoman simply because my eyes have been opened and I see the true madness of the world to which the slaves and their masters refer as "just the way things are," deep down I know that I'm superior to him, because I am able speak with cats, I am able to—

If you don't stop fooling around at once, I'll put you in an asylum, I warned her sternly. And my threat appeared to work, for Mama at last fell silent.

FIFTEEN

The lull didn't last long. Because the process-server, who had just approached the bookcase to the left of the window, had the untimely idea of picking up the statuette of a bare-breasted African woman dressed simply in a raffia skirt who was depicted leaning against a palm tree, which enjoyed pride of place on the said bookcase. My mother immediately threw herself on him, tearing the statuette from his hands. For a moment I was afraid that in her fury she might smash it. But, contrary to expectations, my mother took infinite care to replace the statuette of the bare-breasted African woman on the bookcase.

I was ten years old, I think, when I gave it to her. In the midst of all the hideous items cluttering up the shop window, it had struck me as the embodiment of travel, the allegorical figure of an unrestrained voluptuousness, of an ideal place to be stranded. I had placed it on the living-room sofa with a postcard on the back of which I had written: *Like every year on this day, a day of joy and happiness, I wish you, my darling mother, a very happy birthday and I promise to love you more than anything in this world.*

Mama remained lost in thought for several moments. This statuette, my dear, she said, reminds me of a party in Venerque, a party that was held many years ago to celebrate motherhood, an unforgettable party, my dear, because it marked for me the end of innocence, by which I mean the end of my blindness.

I was six years old. But even now I can see, as if it were
yesterday, the platform in the multipurpose room at the *Foyer
Rural*, all decked out with foliage. I can still see the huge
banner in the colors of the French flag carrying the inscription
JUST ONE LEADER MARSHAL PÉTAIN and the poster
overhanging it depicting six chubby-cheeked, fair-haired
cherubs surrounding like a bouquet of flowers their Madonna-
faced mother. And, my dear, I can see the Jadre twins, drunk
with pride, standing guard on either side of the platform, their
large berets flattened on their heads, making them look like a
pair of oversized mushrooms. I can still see, with incredible
clarity, the white dress I was wearing that day, gathered at my
waist by a blue ribbon, and the red shoes, the ends of which
my mother, your grandmother, had clipped so they wouldn't
pinch my toes.

I can see, one by one, all my classmates grouped to the left
of the platform and arranged in rows according to height. On
the right I can see Venerque's village orchestra, flanked by two
war veterans brandishing the French flag, its pole wedged, no
doubt painfully, in their groins. I can see the notables lined up
along a table installed in the middle of the stage: in the center,
the Mayor, a red-white-and-blue scarf pinned to his massy
chest, surrounded by Madame Duvert, the Departmental Del-
egate to the French Union for the Defense of the Race, Madame
Vérine, Member of the Regional Association for Christian
Marriage, Abbott Vincent, Chairman of the Association for
the Improvement of Public Morals, and Monsieur Perrachon,
Vice-Chairman of the Regional Alliance against Depopulation,
a sly and repellent creature who looked rather like this man
here, she said with a grimace, pointing at the process-server,
the same hypocritical face, she added for good measure.

Mademoiselle gave the signal, one, two, and we lustily broke into *Maréchal nous voilà* . . . "Maréchal here we stand before you the Savior of France," and for once Renée Denjean did not sing in her angel's voice, "Maréchal here we stand before you, both feet in the shit," as we were fearing she might.

We fell silent.

And the procession of mothers advanced into the room. It was a sublime moment and I prayed that nobody would notice the absence of your grandmother, who had not been herself for quite some time already and who had told me the previous day, Take part in that masquerade? I'd rather die. She was, my dear, as obstinate as you are.

After greeting all those present, the Mayor introduced Madame Vérine, who noisily cleared her throat, then, in an indignant voice, her nostrils quivering:

Ladies, gentlemen, my dear children, let us no longer give our favors and our applause to the depraved music-hall divas, to the divorced film stars (I was mad about Danielle Darrieux), to all those outrageously painted ladies with their shaven legs (your grandmother shaved her legs) and those short-haired dimwits (your grandmother wore her hair short) whose scandals fill the pages of the libertarian press. Let us no longer tolerate the trampling and mockery of chastity, dedication, and self-sacrifice (virtues which give women the right to be lethally boring, your grandmother used to say). If at an early age our little girls begin the exercises in moral gymnastics recommended by our venerated Maréchal so that they can forget themselves and think only of others, they will soon learn how to practice quite naturally the cardinal virtues of self-denial and renunciation (the virtues of ugly women, your grandmother said). Mothers of Venerque, all you who hear me, encourage your daughters to attend the home economy classes that Madame Fillol teaches in the main room at the Village Hall, where they will learn how to sew, how to cook and how to submit to their conjugal duty (which consists, your grandmother said, in letting themselves be fucked once a month, so their husbands don't consort with whores, who are expensive). In those days, Mama commented, whores cost much more than they do now. You who know what things are worth, how much does a prostitute cost nowadays? she inquired of the process-server who, punctilious as nobody else could be, was carefully counting the folk dolls which we had long collected. He remained silent. It seemed the matter was not within his competence. A shame. For to me it was of very great interest.

The room burst into applause, my mother continued, and to everyone's surprise, since the organizers had kept quiet about this performance, Monsieur Carloteau, the ironmonger, leapt onto the podium amid a drum roll, wearing tails and trousers that stopped half way down his legs, and holding in his hand some colored scarves. A storm of laughter greeted his appearance, but Monsieur Carloteau wasn't so easily put off. Looking dumbfounded and gesturing emphatically, he began to jerk his scarves around in time with a Viennese waltz, making them fly about in all directions so that the audience could see that each was of a uniform color. As soon as he had begun his incomprehensible simpering and gesticulating, the entire audience once again erupted in laughter which, as you may well imagine, was not at all the reaction anticipated. Even the Mayor began to laugh, so all the notables surrounding him also began to laugh, and even Madame Vérine proved quite

unable to suppress a series of hiccups, causing the chicken
skin around her neck to tremble and ripple. Monsieur Carloteau, however, abandoning none of his misunderstood-seer's
composure, hid the colored scarves behind his huge ass and,
after many theatrical moves, many surprised and curious looks
(produced simply by opening his eyes very wide), slowly drew
from his right sleeve a blue, white, and red flag and from his
left sleeve a square piece of cloth bearing the image of, can
you guess who? of Marshal Pétain, and the crowd again burst
into applause. Monsieur Carloteau returned to his place in
the hall, still wearing his seer's outfit. Larzillière went over to
congratulate him and declared, You made us piss ourselves
we were laughing so hard, a compliment which unleashed a
further uproar and fresh waves of hilarity.

The Mayor, who did not wish the ceremony to turn
into a circus, beat his fist on the table with the authority of
a leader, thus causing all the notables who had been leaning
their elbows thereon to leap up in fright, which unleashed yet
further laughing. Then, with the powerful hand of a gladiator,
he seized the mike and, bringing it close to his large red face:

Our Maréchal, he thundered, for the Mayor had a very
powerful voice, our Maréchal has buried the old Republic,
which was born in the blood of assassination and survived by
sowing hatred, persecuting religion and betraying the Fatherland. Our Maréchal has restored to the priests the freedom
to teach, which Jews and Freemasons had stolen from them,
and has put God back where He belongs, in the schools
from which He had been most ignobly chased. In short, our
Maréchal has undertaken the Cyclopean task (Cyclopean
had a fine ring to it) of ushering in a National Revolution.
We have therefore more than enough reasons to stand and

proclaim at the top of our lungs Vive le Maréchal, and the entire hall stood and proclaimed at the top of its lungs, Vive le Maréchal.

It was now the turn of Monsieur Perrachon who enumerated, one after another, the true values of life as advocated by the Maréchal, prominent among which was: frugality, and there my heart leapt with joy, my dear, for the very least one could say was that your grandmother, your uncle and I lived in a state of exceptional frugality, and my joy was further augmented when Monsieur Perrachon declared that one had to rid oneself of the filthiest, the most miserable and the most anti-Catholic influence of all: that of money, and from that point of view we were—your grandmother, Jean, and I—living paragons. And so have we remained, Mama said proudly to the process-server who failed to react, absorbed as he was in his scribbling, or pretending to be.

Thereupon the village orchestra resolutely struck up an anthem that was at last recognizable as *La Marseillaise*, and at Mademoiselle's signal, one, two, we sang at the top of our lungs the Maréchal's favorite couplet: *Amour sacré de la Patri-i-e conduis soutiens nos bras vengeurs*, and this time Renée Denjean refrained from braying like a donkey *de la patri-eee-ong*, a witticism that ordinarily would make us die laughing, but this was not the moment to fool around.

Abbot Vincent's address, which then followed, was brief but intense:

We lived until now, he began, from day to day, like animals, I would even say lidibi—lididi—excuse me, libibi . . . libidinously. Then came our Maréchal who, as our great poet Paul Claudel has written, leaned down to us and spoke to us as a father, and we then rediscovered the true eternal values of which you, Mothers of France, are the guardians, for you have managed to preserve your children from sick ideas and promiscuity, you have kept from their innocent eyes those odious books that would spread a torrent of debauchery and licentiousness and, thanks to you, Mothers of France, the redeeming love of the Fatherland has been resurrected. I therefore ask you, my dear children, to obey your dear mothers, who are here with you today (would they notice that my mother stood out by her absence? it was all I could think of) and to follow the precepts of our venerable Maréchal (to whom your grandmother in private referred as an old fuck, an old fool, an old bastard and I'll leave it there).

In the crowd, mothers wiped away tears of emotion as applause crackled and spluttered anew.

The Mayor, seeing that time was not standing still, handed the mike to Madame Duvert who, with ecumenical ardor, exhorted the mothers to go forth and multiply, in short to have children in line with an exponential growth curve (which translates as six to eight to the litter) for, she bawled, raising children is a source of joy (especially the wiping of their asses, your grandmother remarked) and it's our national duty to reconstruct eternal France, mother of the arts and much else that's outstanding.

Madame Duvert, electrified, then launched into a eulogy on the glorious virtue of obedience. It is as if all these speeches, my dear, were indelibly printed in my head. Take as an example our Venerated Marshal, she cried in a voice that quivered and quavered, he who has spent his whole life obeying others. As a child he obeyed his mother Clothilde and his father Omer, as an adolescent he obeyed his teachers at the École Saint-Cyr, as an adult he obeyed his military leaders, then in the radiant and glorious autumn of his life, he obeyed the most powerful of the powerful, the Führer in person, and it is this that has made him an awe-inspiring character admired by all. For, Ladies, Gentlemen, my dear children, our Maréchal had the wisdom to obey our German conquerors who are not at all but not at all like what some people say, they can say what they like, the German soldiers are all very polite young men and I know some people, I'll name no names, who would do well to model themselves on them.

The Mayor waited for the applause to die down, tapped on his lips to hide a yawn that puffed out his nostrils and announced that there was a prize of 20,000 francs for a family from Venerque that had seven or more children. He then stood up, an enormous man, and with a pontifical air extracted a piece of paper from his pocket, and the prize goes to, paused for effect, to the Midon family, and the entire room was relieved because the Midon family were in competition with the Espitalier family who were dirty, messy and never paid their debts on time.

Monsieur and Madame Midon, looking extremely intimidated, clambered onto the podium. The Mayor exhorted their children to join them. And the seven Midon children then filed onto the stage, stiff and embarrassed at being exhibited in this way in their paupers' clothes, it was pitiful to behold. The Mayor whispered in Monsieur Midon's ear that it was his duty to make a little speech, go on, go on, be brave, but Monsieur Midon, shambling, his eyes staring, managed only to stammer, Thank you very much, and the seven Midon children felt ashamed for their father for failing to come up with a compliment befitting the occasion. The Mayor, whose disappointment was etched on his face for all to see, waved them away with a flourish of his hand then, in a thunderous voice:

Mothers of Venerque, mothers of prisoners, mothers of martyrs, glorious mothers, long-suffering mothers, Thank you we cry, thank you with all our heart, you who teach our children the eternal virtues, prudence, obedience, and hard work (Does a virtue that makes you unhappy deserve the name of virtue? your grandmother wondered), and above all others, sparkling like a diamond, the virtue of virtues: the sense of sacrifice (it has been confirmed that malice grows hand-in-hand with the sense of sacrifice, she added).

This was the last word and the audience responded with an ovation.

That evening, Inspector, my mother said to the process-server, who was undertaking a meticulous examination of a sideboard containing the odds and ends that served us as crockery, that evening, after the party was over, when I returned to my mother, I was suddenly struck by the fact that her words were out of line with the speeches delivered in the multipurpose room at the *Foyer Rural* during recreational evenings and galas to the glory of motherhood, speeches which were highly edifying, highly bombastic, highly virtuous, and liberally peppered with a kind of fine-sounding epithet that was quite absent from my mother's lexicon.

As you may well imagine, this observation filled me with anxiety.

In that miserly and unfriendly village where she shut herself away, I had the dark premonition, Monsieur, that my mother was infringing upon the governing dogmas and that these were extreme and would brook no violation.

I tried to warn her. She laughed. Her recklessness astounded me. You are out of line, I said, or something of that sort. Make an effort to conduct yourself in a more seemly manner.

But instead, with every day that passed, her behavior grew more scandalous (to the extent that any out-of-the-ordinary behavior scandalizes those whom fear alone, elevated to the status of a doctrine, can hold united), until that fatal day when she walked into the tobacco dealer's and shouted Heil Putain! while doing the Nazi salute. It was this act, Inspector, that condemned my brother to death.

SIXTEEN

And as she said these words, my mother went up to Uncle Jean who, in his frame above the dresser, was gazing down at us with a serious look on his face. Of all the piously preserved portraits that we had of Uncle Jean, this was the largest. It had been taken by grandmother the day of his eighteenth birthday, using a film she had obtained in exchange for some clothing coupons, a dozen eggs, and a kilo of potatoes. In the photograph, Uncle Jean, sitting side-on in a potbellied armchair, was looking straight ahead with those eyes that were so gentle they almost hurt you to look at them and all the grave candor of teenagers who write verse.

Don't touch that, shouted my mother so shrilly that the process-server was halted in his tracks, frozen to the spot.

I was wary of intervening. It was absolutely vital to prevent Mama from having another of her screaming fits. Yet a tactless remark or a word out of place might suffice to trigger a series of seismic shocks leading to the final cataclysm. What I dreaded more than anything was that Mama and the process-server might argue and come to blows. My mother was quite capable of that. She was capable of anything. Even of the worst things you can think of. Especially of those. She had proved it many times.

But nothing happened. With infinite care, Mama removed from its hook the frame in which Uncle Jean reposed, and stood there at length contemplating his face. How beautiful he is, my Jean, he looks like you, my dear, he has your eyes, he died at the summit of his beauty and perfection, is it fortunate that it was so? sometimes I think it is, and for a moment this thought consoles me.

The image of him that will remain engraved in my memory all my life, she said as she pressed a kiss to his paper forehead, for one only keeps, whatever one's feelings are toward the dead, one only holds on to three or four snapshots of them, a trembling smile, a familiar gesture, the madness of a look that lasts but a few seconds, everything else disappears, my dear, however hard one tries to cultivate their memory as I myself strive to do, following the advice that Plutarch gave to Apollonius, everything else, my dear, disappears whatever one does. The image of Jean that remains with me is not this one but another in which, stooping low over a map of Louisiana, as over a cradle, he silently descends the Mississippi of his dreams, one elbow leaning nonchalantly on the rail of a paddle-steamer.

For your uncle, my dear, had traveling in his soul. He dreamed of discovering the India of cows and ecstasies, the sublime cruelties of Mexico, the broad rivers of America, its deserts vast as oceans and the gigantic and miraculous fortunes that were to be had there and with which he would one day shower us, it was promised. But of all his dreams of travelling, there was one that was particularly dear to him, that of going down the Mississippi, leaning on the rail of a paddle-steamer and hailing its sun-drenched banks and cotton fields complete with toiling Negroes, and it is in tribute to this journey that my brother never made, except in his dreams, that I gave you the name Louisiane, as if you were, in some sense, my dear, his geographical child.

My mother fell silent a few seconds while the process-server inexorably pursued his inventory without realizing that what he was thus making was an inventory of our memories, our disappointments, our bitter regrets and our remorse, an entire history, the objects of which bore marks that only we could read.

No one can say, resumed my mother in a voice that tore at my heart, how your grandmother endured life after finding your Uncle Jean the following morning on the railway line, his eyes gazing into the abyss, and his body in pieces like that of a dog killed on the highway, but his face intact and as though delivered from life's worries. Two days after his death, there were just four of us following his coffin to the Saint-Paul cemetery, your grandmother, the village priest, the altar-boy and myself. The curtains in the windows twitched as we passed by. The very walls were oozing fear. That day your grandmother remained standing, did not weep, and performed the trance-like gestures that were expected of her.

But, my mother said, what I can bear personal witness to is the fact that, in the months and years that followed, I lived alongside a woman who both was and was not my mother. For your grandmother, my dear, continued to dig her garden, feed the hens with our excrement, and go about her housework just as she always had done, but she was lacking something, I don't know what, a halo, a nimbus, a flame that had once formed part of her being.

Your grandmother continued to spend her days bent over her sewing machine. She continued to pin together her pieces of cloth and to whipstitch their edges with a hand that had now begun to tremble, she continued to cut the thread with a sharp snap of her teeth, yet there was some indefinable absence within her, an absence that overwhelmed me with worry, an absence that had opened up like a gulf within her and into which, it seemed, her entire life was pouring.

And if I asked her a question, she would give me a look that seemed to soar far beyond earthbound things, a look that went through me without seeing me, fixed as it was on a distant horizon filled with ghosts and horrors, and she would answer me as my mother once used to, but with words devoid of soul, I don't know how to explain all this to you, my dear, with words that were dead.

Some days, she seemed all of a sudden to discover me at her side, I who spent all my Thursdays sitting on a stool between her and the wicker dummy with which I would play, spinning it round on its stand. Then she would ask me to take a knife and scrape away the fluff that had collected in the fold of a hem, because one of the jobs that your grandmother did in those days was to turn clothes inside out so they would appear newer, and I would do my best to de-fluff them, scarcely moving, speaking low, and barely breathing, in the constant fear that the slightest draught might revive the sorrow of this woman, who in spite of everything was still my mother. But I would have given anything, my dear, for her to touch me, for her to hug me in her arms and clasp me to her belly and call me my baby, my love, my beauty, my little dove, as before, or to strike me, to insult me, anything, dear God, just to make me feel like I existed.

I lived, my dear, like a shadow, not knowing what to do with the shadow that I was, not knowing where to go, given that I was prohibited from entering the bedroom that we had formerly shared, Jean and I, and that had now become a somber mausoleum.

I was cold. I suffocated. I wandered sadly from the living room to the garden without finding, in this dead house, a corner where I could just daydream.

Then, sometimes, I would run and take refuge with Filo, in the shed that served as her apartment and that she shared with the hens, the spiders and a rabbit with red eyes that she kept in the oven of a cooker that she had turned into a hutch. Filo caressed me with her tender voice, *Anda hija, no sufras, mañana será otra día*, Come girl, don't suffer, tomorrow's another day. She almost always found some soothing words to say. Do you want to hear about Filo? Mama asked the process-server as he was jotting in his notebook: gilt-plated metal light fitting with six stems ending in five tulip-shaped cones made of white opaline glass. Filo, Monsieur, was a real character. I loved her.

Filomena, Filo to her intimates, had been born in Fatarella, behind I don't know how many mountains, in Spain. She had left her village on foot on January 6, 1939, and landed with us after a month's internment at the camp in Argelès-sur-Mer. One February morning she had taken the first train out of the station, got off in Venerque because after all she had to get off somewhere, and wandered round the village streets for several days looking for a job, knocking on doors which were all slammed in her face. It was Jean who brought her home and Mama who took her in for a day or two on condition she helped out in the garden and with the housework.

She stayed for six years.

Filo taught my mother to make tortillas the Spanish way, to spice up rice which in France tended to taste like plaster, to sing with a Spanish accent *bésame bésame mucho como si fuera esta noche la última vez*, "kiss me kiss me kiss me as if tonight were the last time," and to utter oaths as long as your arm and even longer, *me cago en la virgen me cago en Dios y me cago en la puta madre que te parió*, "fuck the Virgin fuck God and fuck that bitch of a mother that bore you," being my mother's favorite, oaths which, in accordance with tradition, one had to utter all in one go and, as it were, without coming up for breath: *mecagoenlavirgenmecagoenDio-symecagoenlaputama-drequeteparió*, oaths that Filo defined as follows: small rockets launched high into the sky without any intention of causing injury or offense but merely with the aim of breaking with the idiocy of ordinary conversation and of opening small cracks in the walls in which laziness normally encloses us.

Filo often said that the French, with the exception of your grandmother and myself, didn't have enough sensitivity in their hearts, not enough music in their souls to appreciate oaths at their true value. It's sad, she used to say, and French culture is the poorer for it.

When it came to swearing, your grandmother and I, however, proved ourselves gifted students. We acquired both the art and the attitude. For swearing is indeed an art, and the Spaniards are its masters.

Filo also initiated us into the pleasure of dirty jokes and obscene stories which she said were considered, south of the Pyrenees, to be signs of a lively wit, whereas to the north they were regarded as vulgar and common. Do you ever tell any, Mr Process-Server?

The process-server, more impassive than Thrasea, pretended he had heard nothing and continued with his inventory of our old stuff, our junk, I thought, because the fact that it was being viewed by a stranger in this way suddenly made me realize that, with the exception of the plaster statue of the African woman, every single one of our possessions was a shocking assault on good taste and on the spirit of art, an insult hurled at the Greek ideal of beauty that Mama claimed to cherish and of which I was, she sometimes said, the flower. At these thoughts, I was overcome with shame.

Filo, Monsieur, my mother said to the process-server, who was persisting in a stubborn silence that was verging on the impertinent, Filo had only one fault: she was obsessed with food. Ever since she had left Fatarella and spent a month feeding on turnips, the mere mention of a tin of sardines would drive her to the edge of despair. Harassed relentlessly by visions of fatty sauces, roasted meats, marinated peppers, stuffed tomatoes, and cakes dripping with cream, all of which drove her chronic hunger to a point of paroxysm, her stomach would often supplant her brain and her meditations on the hypothetical arrival of chocolate at Legoumaut's the grocer's would prevail over every metaphysical consideration. One day, she wrote a letter to Putain that my mother, fortunately, intercepted and which stated the following: Monsieur le Maréchal, since you are the Master of France and consequently the Master of chocolate, coffee, and vitaminized cakes, would you be so very kind as to send me some, which I would put to the very best possible use?

But, my mother said, when evening came, I would have to leave Filo and her Gargantuan dreams and return to the side of a wild, staring woman whom I called Mama, in this grief-stricken house where . . .

SEVENTEEN

I surrendered to a sudden fit of sadness. My mother's memories affected me more than was reasonable. I came close to sobbing. But I pulled myself together. Unlike my mother, I was not ready to gush shamelessly at the slightest provocation. Among my other qualities, I was endowed with self-control. A great asset.

I choked back my tears. Sniffed discreetly. But on blowing my nose I made an extremely inelegant trumpet-like sound. I who for hours past had been displaying the manners of a princess (princesses, as is well known, never blow their noses), I'd ruined everything.

I'm feeling sad, don't ask me why, I said to the process-server, who hadn't asked me anything, I wouldn't know what to say.

The sadness that was creeping up on me was not unalloyed. A multitude of painful feelings that had arisen since that morning and that I had striven as best I could to suppress suddenly converged. Anger. Humiliation. Shame. The pain of being torn between two warring inclinations: the determination to appear in every way compliant, opposed by the no less tenacious urge to chuck the whole thing in: the process-server, my mother, this entire mess. The exhaustion resulting from my efforts at urbanity, in which, I confess, I had had no training—forgive me, go right ahead, after you, likewise I'm sure—all this bowing and scraping had quite literally worn me out, the constant concern caused by my mother's bad behavior which I was quite unable to moderate even for a second, her outbursts, her yelling, her rages, her revoltingly tasteless jokes, followed by her interminable remorse, her shouting at night, which petrified me, and her terrors which, by an inexplicable process of chemistry, she had instilled in me, her obsessive questions that burrowed their way into my head like moles, precisely like moles, and this feeling of solitude which for months and years had never, as it were, left me.

I'm feeling a little low-spirited, I said to the process-server in whose face I thought I spied a trace of emotion, a frown, a *parpadeo*, as Filo might have said in her genial language. Forgive me, Mr Process-Server, for burdening you with my moods. Listening to me is not, I suppose, covered by your job description. Do you ever get really low? I asked him, and I tried to imagine him in his pajamas on his bed sobbing and passionately kissing his pillow, calling it my love, my sweetie, my darling little whore, then jerking off with desperate ardor. Sometimes, you see, I feel terribly alone. Do you know that feeling?

The process-server gave me one of those looks of his, cold and quick to calculate the price of things, and I had the sensation that in his expert eyes I wasn't worth that much. Was he listening to me? His face remained so unfathomable I simply couldn't say. Perhaps, I reasoned, this process-server just pretended to be as cold as a glacier whereas in actual fact his heart was yearning for love and cried out all day long though nobody could hear it. Perhaps he was secretly hoping that I would throw myself at him, that I would feel him up and clutch him lovingly to my breasts, then, while I was about it, that I would lead him away to fornicate, as is expected. Perhaps he kept concealed beneath that iron mask an exquisite sensitivity, an abstract face, what am I talking about? a surly face more like, what am I talking about? a cruel face, this being essential, given that his job compelled him to undertake tasks which, it seemed clear to me, must be highly unpopular.

Perhaps he was thinking about the scratch he had noticed that very morning on the righthand wing of his Opel Corsa and that had annoyed him greatly.

Perhaps he feared I would manipulate him with my sweet-talking and paralyze him in the concentric spires of my sorcerer's charms, reducing him to nothing.

Perhaps he had expended all his emotions in a former life-time, before becoming a process-server and exposing himself to every kind of rejection, his heart shut as tight as any convent door.

Don't you say anything? Don't you think anything? I inquired.

Unless, quite simply, this process-server thought nothing, felt nothing, unless he were dead, though still living, acting and persevering resolutely in his state of non-being. It was possible. A number of similar cases had been brought to my notice.

Perhaps his apparent coldness was inversely proportional to the depth of his emotions, as is observably the case for example in the German-speaking part of Switzerland and in the countryside surrounding the city of Lille.

Having waited a few minutes for a reply to these several questions and, seeing that none was forthcoming, I'm in need of love, I said to him, just like that.

The process-server resumed his note-taking, thereby giving me to understand that I should keep such inappropriate feelings to myself. But I cared nothing for that, so great was my need to open myself up to another soul.

Without wishing to take up your time, Mr Process-Server, it does seem important to me to bring to your attention the fact that the only humans I see apart from my mother are Nelly and Jawad. Sometimes Nelly phones me and I go down to the sixth floor and we go off together to meet Jawad at the café-bar in the shopping mall. My relations with them are not always easy, it's true, but what relations are easy, can you tell me?

How are you? Jawad asks.

Struggling along, I say.

He splits his sides.

I've scarcely sat down and Jawad's already telling me a dirty joke. Do you know the one about the canary that fucks a . . .

It's always the same thing, Monsieur. I've scarcely sat down and right away I have to endure the bullying coarseness of Jawad who exploits my innocent embarrassment and my chronic inability to understand anything having to do with sex to ridicule and laugh at me. She didn't get it, Jawad says, I don't believe this! In any case, Jawad says, it isn't until a girl has held a cock in her hands that she understands anything about anything. Against which I protest. I respond that to renounce love or cock, as you put it, does not mean you have to forego the pleasures of Venus, on the contrary it is to enjoy their advantages without being held ransom, and thereby to attain an inner state of ataraxia that brings us closer to God, I've read this in Callimachus.

You what? What? Jawad can't believe his ears. Would you mind speaking plainly? Honestly, I don't believe this! Who's this fucking Galli-mackus? I've never heard of the guy! You're totally out of your mind, you're just like your mother. And as I'm on the verge of bursting into tears, Never mind, darling, Jawad says feeling sorry, you're bound to get laid one of these days, don't cry Loulou, you too shall have your love story, but just one thing, above all make quite sure you don't get laid by some poverty-stricken jerk-off, make quite sure before he screws you that he's carrying a credit card and that it's really his.

I have to admit, to be perfectly honest with myself, that Jawad's bullying, often approved and even encouraged by Nelly, doesn't bother me quite as much as I have implied. And to tell the truth, Nelly and Jawad are the only people in the world who assist me in my slow, my arduous, my painful, my laborious, my impossible progress toward the affairs of love.

Jawad tells Nelly a joke. She laughs. Serge, the waiter in the café-bar, spins his tray like a top on the tip of one of his fingers. Serge reminds me of one of the Jadre twins, I say, just to say something. Of who? asks Nelly, who's on her third beer and isn't paying attention. You know, the story about the twins who ball these two sisters, Jawad tells Nelly, there's these two guys and they're twins and they . . .

Nelly and Jawad fall over laughing, that's a really good one. They order another beer and a sandwich. Then they decide to go to the movies. Since I don't have a centime on me, I pretend I'm not sure about the film. I assume an air of indifference. Action movies, you know . . . Come on, I'll pay yours, Jawad says. I'm still not sure, I say, more feebly now. I have my pride. Come on, force yourself a little, my little Loulou, Jawad says, you've got to get some education, education's important. So I force myself.

The fact is that I love going to the movies with Nelly and Jawad. For them, a cinema is a bedroom. Even though they don't perform, in the strict sense of the term, the act of fornication, Nelly and Jawad get into some pretty astounding holds which I monitor furtively. Nelly pounces on Jawad and begins working, if I may put it like this, from the bottom up, opening her mouth very wide, opening her mouth much wider than I would have believed possible, while Jawad puffs and blows like a seal, do seals puff and blow? while Jawad pants. Then, all of a sudden, his head drops forward, inanimate and gasping, and Nelly, disheveled and scarlet, sits back up in her chair with a sidelong glance, half dignified and half ashamed, while a magnificent Mel Gibson falls prey *in extremis* to the generous, and sexually promising, love of Sophie Marceau: two shows for the price of one.

I observe, to my utter amazement, that the unquestionable tokens of love that Nelly and Jawad have been exchanging cease the instant they walk out the cinema doors. No more cuddling. No more frenzy. No more bliss. Just endless mockery and teasing that pits the one against the other in an extreme rapture, as though this were the natural continuation, in I don't know what twisted way, of the fleshly pleasures they had tasted while kissing, unless, following the filthy behavior in which they have just so avidly indulged, such mockery serves to rehabilitate, that is to say to purify, their souls, avid as they are for the Infinite, how beautiful that is, how beautiful.

Where was I, Mr Process-Server? I have the impression I've strayed from the heart of my subject. My mother? I'm coming to her.

After the movies, I return home. There I find my mother, unchanged, with her sorrow, unchanged, and her ravings, unchanged. I prepare her evening remedies: a tablet of Artane, one of Tranxene, another of Largactil and fifty drops of Haldol. Kill or cure.

At eight o'clock sharp, we watch the TV news. During the day, Mama and I move along lines that are tangential, each one locked in her bedroom, each one nailed down in front of her TV set, Mama with her head saturated with fantastic visions which she projects on the screen, and me quite empty filling myself up with empty images, Mama enthused and vehement, her eyes turned inward, me bored, morose, my spirit sagging: I oversimplify, but not much.

But at eight o'clock sharp, we converge on the living-room settee. It's a ritual. I don't have the courage to break it. We settle down side by side in front of the TV set which becomes from that moment on the center of our mental gravitations.

Have I already expounded to you, my mother says, my theory of ghosts?

I pretend I'm listening to her.

Ghosts exist, she begins, I have collected in a matter of days the twelve proofs of their existence. Hold on tight, I tell myself. You don't believe in them? she asks. Sure I do, Mama, sure I do. They wander around facelessly, Mama says, shrouded in black veils, and mingle with the living without anyone noticing them, because ghosts, unlike us, are non-voidable and non-evictable, she adds, humorously. They go where they like. They pass through walls and cross frontiers at their leisure. (In a neutral tone of voice, the news anchor announces a new crime in Algeria). Today they're in Algiers, as the report makes clear, tomorrow they'll be in Egypt, they visit places that reek of death, and there are plenty of places on the planet that reek of death, that can't be denied. (The news anchor announces the discovery of a scene of carnage in Rwanda). You wonder who they are and where they come from, my dear. Ghosts are the dead whom Putain and his gang have murdered and who rise again and come watch us live. She's off again, I say to myself, in great dismay. Ghosts come and watch us live, and that's all it takes to wreak such havoc. Do you understand, my dear?

I understand nothing. The views I have on life and the world are secular and Cartesian. And I intend to hold onto them. I believe neither in signs nor in divinations. And every form of supernaturalism makes me want to laugh. I understand, Mama, I understand, I tell her anyway. (The news anchor announces an increase in the price of cigarettes. That's hardly calculated to cheer me up.)

And what if you took care of the living? I say to her. I have a treacherous side. What are you insinuating? Mama asks me. I decide not to press the issue. So she resumes: Burying the dead is not enough to erase their existence, my dear, for their immortal souls always return to us under one guise or another, sometimes taking the form of a noise that only a few very well-informed people, like Sophocles or myself, know how to hear, at other times assuming the shape of the living, but how then can one tell the dead from the living? Mama cries out, worried all of a sudden, then jumping up and touching my face to satisfy herself that it is warm and moves, Are you there, my dear? are you living? answer! I'm here, calm down. She does calm down, but then she's off again at once, Crimes that are unforgiven spawn fresh crimes, she utters in a voice whose prophetic tones give me goose bumps. The present, my dear, is infinitely contaminated by the past, our memories are crushed beneath a weight of filth, the bourgeois do their quiet counting in the midst of furies, the Earth has become a vast cemetery on which Putain and his pimps build profitable parking lots, and she could go on for hours complaining like this, with an unending stream of terrible words, if I didn't switch off the TV at eleven to avoid Madame Darut, whose soul is unreceptive to nocturnal elegies, from banging with her broom on the dividing wall, and screaming Shut up, you screwballs!

We go to bed.

The days pass.

We remain alone together, each enclosed in a deadly solipsism.

Are you wondering, Mr Process-Server, what use we make of our days, apart from our prolonged sessions in front of the TV screen? To be blunt: none.

I remain in the living room, which is also my bedroom. I smoke a cigarette. I look at myself in the mirror. I decide I'm ugly. I put black eyeliner round my eyes, gel on my hair, and foundation on my forehead to cover my spots. I turn on the TV. I'm bored to death. This is not a life, I say to myself. Except that it is. I feel overcome by galloping inertia. Isn't that, Mr Process-Server, what one calls an oxymoron? I say, to make myself interesting. The urge is too strong, I can't help playing the cultivated lady, I have the impression that it erases all the rest: the spots on my face, the cheap clothes I wear, my empty purse.

Sometimes, Monsieur, a spasm of anxiety grips my chest, it really hurts. I lie down on my bed. I feel as if I'm sinking. I'd like to be somewhere else, in Malaga, with Nelly and Jawad, listening to their obscene jokes and laughing to myself. At six o'clock I watch my soap on Channel Two. At seven o'clock I watch my soap on Channel One. I prefer the latter. The leading actor has dark hair and green eyes and I like men with dark hair and green eyes. I have no other activities. It seems there are quite a number of us in this situation.

I do nothing at all, Monsieur, that's the truth of it. And Mama encourages me to persevere amid this nothingness. What's important is to persevere, she says, and perseverance in one's resolutions is a great thing. Seneca says, says Mother, that idleness, when it's persistent, is a virtue. Mama knows what she's talking about, she never lifts her little finger, hence the terrible mess, Mr Process-Server, that you can observe with your own eyes and for which I sincerely beg your forgiveness.

Are you wondering how on earth we manage to make ends meet? We get by on very little. That's our secret. I say it with some pride: nobody could live more cheaply than we do. Three thousand francs a month for two people, who could do better? There's something miraculous about it, isn't there? Something that provides great hope for future generations! My mother, it has to be emphasized, is not motivated by the lust for money which, as you well know, is innate in the human soul. Mama, through some aberration wholly unknown to me, has transmuted her lust for money, into what? into madness, without any doubt. There is no other explanation. Which accounts for a great many of our tribulations. But let's not overstate it.

The fact is, Mr Process-Server, that all I do is loaf . . . that is, I spend my entire day in a state of idleness that my mother encourages. For my mother claims, Monsieur, that *praxis* takes us away from *being*. To work is to surrender to the enemy, that's what she maintains, it is to make a deal with the devil (such glittering words she uses!) and to risk submitting to the quarrels of those more mediocre than ourselves.

Besides, all employers are supporters of slavery, which, she asserts, is a fact that is insufficiently known. All of which, you see, is scarcely designed to spur me on to labor, nor indeed to any of the other civic activities so much appreciated by the French.

And as if the process-server suddenly felt remiss for allowing himself to be unduly distracted, he resumed his official process-server's behavior, refocused his process-server's gaze, which seemed to turn objects and beings to ice and, having consulted his process-server's watch, considering no doubt that things were dragging a little, asked Might I visit the room at the back?

EIGHTEEN

I rushed at once into my mother's bedroom, sprayed air-freshener all around to disperse the putrid stench, threw open the windows that my mother, for fear of spies, kept permanently closed, grabbed hold of some raggedy clothes left lying on a chair and threw them into the cupboard, while at the same time kicking under the bed some few of the hundreds of books that littered the floor.

Be so kind as to come in, I said. I couldn't be any nicer, and I must admit I was developing a taste for it.

Stepping over an initial heap, the process-server entered Mama's bedroom, skidded on a mound of newspapers, picked his way between columns of books, piles of discarded clothing, a scattering of papers, empty bottles and, at the conclusion of an obstacle-strewn expedition, estimated the value of an inlaid bedside table with a marble top, a bedside rug depicting a tiger in shades of black and white against a blue background decorated with arabesques, a bed with chromium metal posts, consisting of a Dunlopillo mattress, measuring 140x190 cm., and a Dunlopillo slatted base, measuring 140x190 cm., When was the purchase of this bed effected? asked the process-server who, in his questions, was completely lacking in imagination.

In 1978, a year before I was born. A date that ushered in a new era, Monsieur, for it was that year that my mother contracted a nervous disorder. Why? Because a certain number of events ignited, as it were, her memory. But I get the impression, Mr Process-Server, from the expression on your face, that you are eager to know the nature of the said events. On October 28, 1978, precisely thirty-five years after the death of her brother, my mother read in *L'Express* an interview that Louis Darquier de Pellepoix, former General Commissar on Jewish Questions, gave to Philippe Ganier-Raymond, an interview during which Darquier de Pellepoix stated that Bousquet and he alone had been responsible for the infamous roundup of Jews in 1942.

It was on reading this interview, Monsieur, on October 28, 1978, at ten o'clock in the morning, that the fate of my mother was sealed. Or her madness. Whichever you prefer.

On October 28, 1978, my mother, who up until then had led a life made up of countless succeeding days all very much the same, of moderate sorrows, of some pleasures but not too many, and some minor disappointments, a life so settled, Mr Process-Server, so routine, that at times she said to herself that it hardly was a life, on that October day my mother became suddenly convinced, as in a revelation, that she had a mission. Who dictated it to her? no one knows. It's my Jean, she would say sometimes in a burst of mysticism, my Jean who is speaking through my mouth and who is talking to God. My mother, I was saying, was convinced she had been assigned a sacred mission, that of revealing in the full light of day the paralipomena of History, all the despicable actions, Monsieur, that official histories leave out, all the infamies concealed beneath the flower-strewn tombs on All Saints Day, the vile tricks with which the State adorns the sacred name of the Fatherland, the lies, the embezzling, the violence, the simony, and the acts of wickedness dolled up with pretty sentiments and pompous adjectives.

And suddenly my mother's life was a life.

She resolved, that very morning, to reinstate the justness in justice, of which, she declared, we had been despoiled, since those supposed to administer it covered their ears, and veiled their faces in shame.

In her incipient madness, she decided to devote all her strength and all her soul to struggling against the spirit of impurity and against those who, in her eyes, embodied it, and Bousquet, she said, was one of them. The time to settle old scores has come and I'm the person who has been appointed to do the job, my mother declared conceitedly, laughing proudly. In its desolation, History has chosen me, she exulted, I who am nothing but a petty postal worker, I can't get over it.

And from that moment on my mother, who wouldn't have hurt a fly, had it in her head to bring to justice the man who in her view had brought the reign of Evil into the World, always such grand phrases she used, and on whom, in the absence of any verdict handed down by the official authorities, she would inflict a punishment in her own way. How? By shooting him in the chest. Simple as that. Don't smile, Mr Process-Server, this is a matter of great seriousness.

In her deranged state of mind, Mama imagined that by getting rid of one man she could cure the world's gangrene at a single stroke and erase the foul stink it had created. Pure madness. She believed that simply by settling Bousquet's account she could settle not only the worm-eaten accounts of History itself but her own. What naivety! One must, she declared, render measure for measure and destroy those who have done us such evil, that's the wise counsel that Hesiod imparts. The future—should we fail to punish the monsters who have left in their wake a country ravaged by shame and death—the future will punish us, and Uncle Jean, and all those like him who died in horror, will die a second time and go on dying forever.

My mother, Monsieur, mistook herself for the Angel of Judgement, even though, it has to be said, she neither looks nor acts the part. She wished single-handedly to make good all the moral shortcomings of an age, if you please! and, armed with a little 6.35 caliber bought from a retired cop, to face down the forces of evil: it was utterly hilarious! for my mother believed in the triumph of the good and the victory of the just, and only the deranged, Monsieur, believe in such bull.

She now spent her days keeping watch outside the Bank of Indochina, of which Bousquet was both Chairman and Director General. She was noticed, changed tactics, and asked an employee to get her an appointment with the big shot. The employee examined her worn-out shoes (from Bata), went and fetched a second employee who examined her (lopsided) chignon, referred her to a third employee who examined her from her worn-out shoes (from Bata) to her (lopsided) chignon and answered her, very dryly, that the Chairman and Director General does not receive anyone with personal requests, but you are of course welcome to mail him.

For an entire year, my mother wrote letter after letter, asking for a meeting which she qualified as business, emphasizing with great eloquence the very particular nature of her case.

It was a waste of time.

So she knocked on the doors of several high-ups whose names I shall not mention but who had rubbed shoulders with Bousquet during his glory days. No door opened. Not to be discouraged, she continued her efforts, indulging in the luxury of lunching at the Chez Paul restaurant of which Bousquet was a habitué, seeking out the best angle from which to shoot him; she even managed, I don't know how, to be present several years running at the Mass offered in memory of Laval in the Chapel of the Maison des Jésuites, an anniversary that Bousquet never missed, and she joined the Association for the Defense of Marshal Pétain, hoping to bump into Bousquet there or somehow gain an insight into his intentions, as it were, from the inside.

My mother ended up knowing everything about Bousquet that there was to know, but none of the details that she discovered revealed to her his secret. She learned that he enjoyed the protection of the President of the French Republic and that consequently she had to watch her step. She learned that he selected his fedoras at Leon's in Place Vendôme, that he had his suits made at Lanvin's, the height of chic, that he wore camelhair overcoats and peccary gloves, the most expensive there were, that he loved wrestling matches commentated by Claude Darget, that he smoked Players filter-tips, drove around in a Mercedes, and lived in a comfortable apartment on Avenue Raphaël. She learned all that and more. But Bousquet's soul remained closed to her. The damning evidence she was looking for existed only in books.

She read all the books, Monsieur, in which his name appeared.

She reread them.

She found out about his childhood, his life's various stages, his acts of glory, his darker moments. She found out that he had been born in Montauban and that his father had been a notary. She found out that he was appointed sub-prefect of police at twenty-six years of age, deputy at thirty-one and government minister at thirty-three, and that his heart was filled with an insatiable lust to succeed. She found out that he possessed a natural and conspicuous elegance, that he liked order, women, dogs and honors. She found out that if he had chosen to allow himself to become corrupt, it was by himself that he had been corrupted and by himself alone.

For years, she rummaged in his past with the jealous zeal of a woman in love.

NINETEEN

But as she dug around in Bousquet's past, all the war-time memories she had stored in the depths of her soul resurfaced higgledy-piggledy, some she had lived through and others she had invented, some were fleeting and nebulous and melted away the moment they appeared, while others were precise, bloody, ghastly, filling her with terror.

All her memories, Monsieur, became entangled in her head, jumbled up with ancient melancholies, the amplified echoes of Jean's screaming, and the latest refinements of horror brought to her all the way from Africa by TV.

Her memories, Monsieur, went berserk.

Her state of mental confusion soon became apparent, alarming Josette and Marceline, her colleagues at the mail office. She was forever talking to them about Bousquet, while concealing the plan she had devised to kill him, sometimes referring to him as the Chief of Police and at other times as the Banker, sometimes declaring that he was in the pay of the Boche and at other times in that, no less ignoble, of Capital, sometimes marveling at his lightning promotion within the government of Vichy and at other times at the cunning, suspicious, and yet blasé sides to his character that made him a peerless financier, without ever ceasing, however, to call him a whore, a *putain*, so that it was often impossible now to tell whether she was talking about Bousquet, Pétain, or another of her enemies, she even got lost herself, she was becoming, Mr Process-Server, completely crazy.

Pouillon, her office manager, called her into his office. She had probably been overworking, a few days rest from work might do the . . .

Rest! You have to be joking, my mother protested. She had quite other concerns on her mind than those occasioned by the delicate state of her health! By this time, Bousquet, to mention only him, was no doubt perusing a letter denouncing a certain Lazare Apfelbaum, as well as a man named Baysse, both of whom lived in Venerque, in the department of Haute-Garonne, and was probably asking Marguerite his secretary to pass the letter on to Monsieur Darquier de Pellepoix, General Commissar for Jewish Questions, who would draw it to the attention of Monsieur Cheneaux de Leyritz, the Regional Chief of Police in Haute-Garonne, who would pass it on to Monsieur Bézagu his Deputy Chief of Police who, in collaboration with Monsieur Boucher his Police Intendant, would then pass it on to the competent authorities who would, it was not to be doubted, take the necessary steps. Try to understand! my mother said, this is rather more important than my aches and pains!

Her manager listened to her story without understanding a single word, but realized that she was much sicker than he had at first suspected. Her madness, which he had believed to be mild, was in fact of the raving variety.

He attempted to reason with her. My mother screamed her head off, A few days vacation! When the destiny of a country is at stake! You can't be serious!

Only this morning, she explained to him (this conversation was taking place in January 1979, approximately one year before I was born), Bousquet travels to Vichy to report back to Putain on his talks with Oberg. It's a date that should be etched in our memories. Ménétrel shows him into the drawing room where the Marshal is waiting for him. Bousquet explains to the Marshal first Oberg's positions and then his own. My firmness on the issue of quotas paid off, Bousquet tells him. What quotas? Pétain asks. The quotas of Jews to be, ah, transferred, Bousquet explains. At this juncture, Ménétrel opens the office door and announces Monsieur Abel Bonnard. Who's he? the Marshal inquires. He has forgotten that Bonnard is his Minister. The Gestapo-Queen, says Ménétrel, who from time to time allows himself a little joke. Tell him to wait outside.

Throughout the rest of the interview, the Marshal dozes, wakes with a start, raises his head, yes? what? asks after Bousquet's family, ignores the reply, falls asleep again, snores thrice, half-opens one eye, asks after Bousquet's son, about whom he couldn't give a damn, nods off, snores slightly, wakes with a start, and your dear wife?

Bousquet repeats each time, with mounting embarrassment, that Raymonde is fine and that his son is quite popular with his classmates. For a brief moment, he thinks Pétain has died. Panic seizes him. He calls for Ménétrel who fails to reply. Then he calms down. Observing the Marshal at close quarters, he can see that his throat is rising with each regular intake of breath. Accordingly he . . .

My mother's manager was by this time confirmed in his opinion. Rose Mélie had gone crazy.

To tell the truth, her madness came and went.

On her good days, Mr Process-Server, my mother was peaceable, inhabited the present, took an interest in the affairs of the world, found amusement in them, was made indignant by them, it all depended. On her bad days, the blood of her tortured memory obscured her spirit, dates grew confused in her head, the Jadre twins, she would cry out in alarm, have pushed an Arab into the Seine, why will they never learn? it's enough to make you despair, and only yesterday, they scrawled their venom on the wall next to our door, in full view of everyone: KICK OUT THE COMMIE. This threat is aimed as much at us as it is at Filo, that much is obvious, the Jadre twins are trying to intimidate us, acting on the orders of You-Know-Who. But that's not going to shut me up, Mama shouted. I'm going to tell everybody about the paralipomena, she shouted (I was getting sick and tired of her paralipomena) and Filo is not going anywhere, I'm not giving in, Filo's not going back to live under Franco, never, never, my dear. I'm afraid the Jadre twins may visit on us the same tortures they inflicted last month on the widow Dastrugue. I have no inclination whatsoever to crawl on all fours on a leash held by those filthy bullies nor, at a snap of their fingers, to prostrate myself at their feet. It'd kill me.

Jean says there's no need to worry, my dear. He'll talk to the Jadre twins on Saturday at the Café des Platanes, before they've drunk too much beer. Jean has a way of finding the right words to touch people's hearts. Yet I dread their meeting. Those twins, my dear, I don't like the look of them at all. Because the Jadre family, you see, she explained to me, do nothing but obey that Putain who governs us and whom I intend to bring to justice. Nobody's going to convince me otherwise.

You have to know, Mr Process-Server, that in her afflicted state of mind, Pétain, Bousquet, Darnand, and the Jadre twins had gradually all blurred into one and the same person whom, for the sake of convenience, she called Putain, a figure whose features were confused, changeable, unstable, and in whom one should see not the embodiment of a mere human being but rather an idea, a symbol: the emblem of evil itself.

I did everything in my power, Mr Process-Server, to restore my mother to a more orthodox pattern of thought. I exhorted her to take care of herself. I appealed to her reason. Every day I erected against her madness great walls of arguments. I objected to her:

– that she had only to take a look at the same history books that she made me read to realize that governments had almost always been in the hands of serial killers. Tiberius, Caligula, Claudius, Nero, have you never heard of these murderers?

– that it might be better if she took some interest in the living. In me, for instance. I piled guilt onto her. My weapon of choice;

– that after all it wasn't my fault if those people had committed atrocities, goddamn it. But, we are always responsible for the murders we inherit, Mama replied, speaking in that sententious tone that I so detest and that she had acquired, I suppose, from her reading of the Bible and classical authors. That's some inheritance! I exclaimed;

– that Putain, whatever she said about him, had none the less been created in our likeness, I mean that he was human, like her and me, well not exactly;

– that she should shut up. Because I'd run out of arguments. And patience.

Some winter evenings, a sadness, dropping on me from the sky or from who knows where, imbued my remarks with an uncustomary profundity. What, I would say to her, is the point of lifting the lid on such a foul stink? And later, Is Putain's soul any more evil than anyone else's? Besides, who are you to declare Putain a monster? An idiot earthworm, conceded my mother, who had read Pascal's *Pensées*. What is the point of compounding a crime and piling sorrow on sorrow? And what will you achieve by killing Putain other than to extend the slaughter by adding a new and equally insane murder, thereby placing yourself on the side of those whom you denounce? In any case, nothing will ever make up for the death of Uncle Jean, nothing, least of all the death of a man, or a hundred men, or a thousand. She fell silent. I triumphed. But not for long.

For on the following day her ravings would begin anew, even more vigorous, more assured, more lushly imaginative, and magnificent. A jungle. Even if I demonstrated to her the absurdity of her plan a hundred times, she still wouldn't drop it. Since everyone else, she said, cowards all, shirked their duty, she would have to take justice into her own hands. No power in the world could dissuade her. None at all. Consider it done.

One unforgettable February evening, February 10, 1979, to be precise, my mother who, as you will have noticed, Mr Process-Server, possesses an unpredictable and wholly incandescent spirit, my mother burst into a TV studio and, seizing hold of a mike, yelled The hour of justice has arrived. (All the show's guests seemed frozen to the spot.) Since Putain has escaped from the righteous wrath of the law, thanks to God only knows what sort of underhand contacts, and remains scandalously unpunished in spite of all his crimes, I myself shall dispense justice. (All the show's guests, welded in their disapproval, had their eyes riveted on the host). There were

148

some who have believed that memory might be muzzled. Well, they can think again! It is I who shall counter this assault on memory. I shall make known all the paralipomena, even with my dying breath, and shall inflict on the guilty the punishment they merit. For it is time, ladies and gentlemen, to stop mincing our words and to call a swine a . . .

But she didn't have time to call her swine the name he deserved, for a security man, sprung from nobody-knew-where, grabbed her by the neck and dragged her off into the wings.

Among the TV celebrities, there was an explosion. Everyone talked at once and at the tops of their voices. They were unanimous in their view: the woman was nuts. But who might this Putain be? They lost themselves in conjecture. Several different hypotheses emerged. The most skeptical claimed there was a *putain*, a whore, lurking behind every politician. You might just as well search for a needle in a haystack.

As for our heroine, my mother, the police drove her to the nearest ER. The following day, Mr Process-Server, she was taken to the Hôpital Sainte-Anne where she was committed. It was the first of a long series of hospitalizations.

TWENTY

It was the Sainte-Anne *concentration camp*, rectified my mother, who had walked into her bedroom and was warily monitoring my confabulation with the process-server. Alleging that I wasn't responsible for my actions, police officers came and took me from the sidewalk like a, well, there isn't a feminine name for assassin, though there should be, like a murderess, let's say. I protested, yelled, scratched and punched, but my resistance only made matters worse for me. I was driven, against my will, to the ER. There I was forcibly administered an injection of Droleptan which immediately deprived me of my ability to think. The following day, a group of white-coated Militia-members transferred me, forcibly, to the Saint Anne internment camp. There, they stripped me, forcibly placed me in a straightjacket, the sleeves of which were twice as long as ordinary sleeves, and knotted them one to the other behind my back just like mad people were treated in barbarous times, then they forcibly locked me in a window-less cell in which all the furniture had been fixed to the floor, they forced me to swallow potions that left me unconscious, literally unconscious, my dear, for I was no longer conscious of anything or anyone except of you for whom I called out in vain, and I felt then that my soul was dropping, nose-diving, into emptiness.

Dr Logos came to my bedside. He had to confirm whether or not, yes or no, by denouncing publicly on television the foul butchery of which Putain was the instigator if not the material perpetrator, whether or not, yes or no, I was responsible for my actions. A vast question, which I shall address later on, my dear, in all the detail that the topic requires. But, just for now, you should know that I was as responsible for my actions as anybody ever has been.

When Dr Logos cast his eyes upon me, I felt that an icy rain was falling on my whole being. How are you? His voice was that of a priest: pink, slippery and smooth. With an undertone of cunning. Have you slept well? He asked me a couple of smooth, anodyne questions, like Militiamen when they are trying to assuage their victims' suspicions and weaken their resistance, just before they throw the electric switch. I wanted to talk, beg him to leave me in peace, but all I could articulate was a formless mash of words that were unintelligible, even to me. Because words, my dear, were no longer mine to use. The words to answer him stuck in my throat. They were so heavy and grave and solemn that the effort needed to haul them up over the wall of my mouth and fetch them all the way to my lips was just too great.

After many days in a stupor, I finally managed to explain to him that an inner order had prompted me to act as I had done, an order that had arisen within me but that was greater than myself, a sort of divine order that had taken me out of my own being, you couldn't possible understand, Doctor, an order that had been dictated to me by a superior yearning, by a supra-individual, I'd even go so far as to say, by a supra-national yearning, for a cause, I emphasized, which was not in any way my own but rather that of humankind in its entirety, no more and no less than that. My mission, I stammered, was to reveal to the world the paralipomena of . . .

I became aware in that instant that that word was too much. It confirmed Dr Logos' diagnosis. *Mystical jargon and ditto delusions.* What a pain!

That day I got no further with the exposition of my grand scheme. Quickly, with the help of other inmates, I came to understand that on no account whatsoever should one open one's heart to Dr Logos and his Militiamen. For it seemed they had the filthy habit of rooting around in any hearts thus opened.

Throughout the next few days, I remained on my guard. I learned to dissemble. Putain? Don't know him. Darnand? Never seen the man. My first shit? My second moment of ecstasy? The state of my urges? Nonsense, nonsense. My father walking out? My mother's melancholia? Out the window! Buried. My main aim was to take cover from the treatment raids with which camp inmates were regularly bombarded, having realized that the remedies proposed by these doctors-to-the-soul were in fact much more harmful than the ills they sought to treat.

In the art-for-nuts workshops, I drew green trees, blue clouds, circular suns and, in the midst of all this, happy families. In the group-therapy sessions, I debated the thorny issue of yogurt flavors: vanilla? chocolate? raspberry? fruits of the forest?

I applied myself to stupidity.

And was successful.

Dr Logos complimented me on my progress.

In the TV room, I met your father, a Spaniard, dark of skin and dark of heart. A gang of extraterrestrials endowed with the gift of ubiquity kept forcing their attentions upon him, weaving plots and perverse machinations of which he was at one and the same time the perpetrator and the victim. He confided in me. We made love. The following day, he called me by a strange name. He no longer knew who I was. A month later, he vanished.

The days passed gloomily. Then one morning I felt the heat of the sun touch my skin like a kiss. The next day, I learned how to laugh again. The day after that, I began to argue.

Three days later, bewildered and amazed, Dr Logos declared me cured.

As soon as I was liberated, I got back to the job of tracking down Putain, so much so that—

So much so, Monsieur, I angrily resumed, turning now toward the process-server, you'd have thought we were in the theater, so much so that for years I had the impression that nothing else existed for my mother, Monsieur, but this Putain who made me so wretched, Putain, Putain, Putain and nobody but him. And as for me, all this while, my mother quite forgot me.

That's not true, Mama yelled.

My mother forgot me, I blared out, dumping me from time-to-time with foster families from whom I always attempted to flee. For my mother, Monsieur, devoted herself body and soul to her sublime scheme and was only briefly aware of me.

You're exaggerating, Mama protested, preferring to leave the room rather than hear what I was about to say. I'm going to the shithouse, she said by way of excuse, as she stepped out of her bedroom. Such an elegant turn of phrase. I wondered what good it did her to read Petrarch. None whatever. None of her reading did her any good. Or perhaps it did. It got her exempted from household chores. And who ended up doing them in her place?

Mama, Monsieur, was only briefly aware of me. Look after me! I begged her. But she was too busy somewhere else, kilometers away, wrapped up in her global plans, at some sublime altitude. Mama, I'm hungry, Mama, I'm thirsty. But she was too busy striding through the mountaintops, campaigning for planetary peace and interracial love. Mama, I'm cold, I'm shivering. But she was too busy reshuffling governments and fighting for the representation of sodomites in government. Mama, I've got a tummy-ache, Mama, I'm telling you I'm hurting. But she was too busy negotiating with ghosts. And quarrelling with Putain. The two of them. Tirelessly.

Until one day I decided, Monsieur, to become my mother's mother. Mama, calm down, please, people are looking at you, don't talk so loud, take a shower, no, it isn't Putain, it's Jacques Dufilho, because I'm telling you it's not Putain, Mama, your drops, fifty, and your three tablets, you say they knock you out? not enough, they don't! Mama, don't go out in that outfit, you're grotesque, Mama, don't do this, don't do that. What would you have done in my place? I asked the process-server who was now concentrating his attention on Mama's TV set (we each had our own) and was jotting down in his little notebook: a color television set, brand Philips, screen 54 cm, multifunctional remote control.

So you want to cart off my TV set, do you? screamed my mother, who had re-entered her bedroom as quietly as a cat. It's a quite excellent idea, Monsieur. The fewer goods, the fewer worries! Besides, those who possess nothing, have lost nothing, it was Seneca who said that and I'm in complete agreement. For the happy man, said Seneca, is not he who has an abundance of goods but he whose goods are locked up in his soul. Take then, Monsieur, that terrible TV set, its nonstop talking exhausts me and teaches me nothing, take all this bric-a-brac, at least this way we will cheat the thieves, take the horrible ornamental cabinet that I inherited from my mother, it's a fake and it gets in my way, take all this furniture that only serves to highlight our wretchedness, take while you're at it these ghosts who hurl reproaches at me even in my nightmares, compelling me to sleep with the light on, take my memories, my sorrows, my foolish illusions, my stupid beliefs, and the voice of my dead, you can take it all, Monsieur, you will never be able to take my desires, it was Epictetus who said that and I agree with him one hundred percent, and my mother continued like this for a long while until the process-server, who had remained, throughout this time, his soul shut tight, his mouth shut tight, announced dryly: I should now like to visit the bathroom.

I didn't much care for his tone of voice, but I did my best to hide my feelings. But certainly, Mr Process-Server, I said. Then I had a moment's hesitation.

TWENTY-ONE

I had a moment's hesitation. Although the bathroom is a place that is unanimously deemed hostile to the conservation of paper, we had turned it, Mama and I, into a little reading room, the bathtub now serving at one and the same time as a wardrobe and a library. Therefore, before proceeding with my tour, I provided an explanatory preamble.

My mother, Mr Process-Server, I put it in precisely these terms, does not submit to the hygienic rules of others. Taking the view that our pussycat Camille is an example to be followed in numerous respects (the feline virtues being, according to my mother, poles apart from the characteristics of the German soul that she abhors), Mama regards herself to be clean once she has very hastily washed her face and some of the neighboring orifices. And when, made uncomfortable by her exhalations, I reprimand her sharply, my mother objects, Monsieur, that in view of the fact that she has long outgrown the stage at which one attaches importance to appearances and that she is no longer called upon to perform any tasks of a degrading and sudoriferous nature, her opportunities for getting dirty are nonexistent. It's untrue, Mr Process-Server. My mother gets dirty and stinks the place up. But she doesn't give a damn. And I'm the only one who suffers from it.

The process-server looked at his watch and reiterated his request to visit the bathroom. I consented. One more humiliation could make no difference. My pride, this repugnant wound forever on the point of reopening, had endured so many affronts since the process-server's arrival that it had, as it were, quite withered away. To hell with pride, I said to myself as I showed the process-server into our little reading room.

After several contortions, the process-server succeeded in squeezing his way through to the washbasin and he began by opening the medicine cabinet which was fully stocked with drugs to treat my mother's illness.

I am duty-bound to admit, I confided to the process-server, that I and Nelly do sometimes make use of these tablets. We go up to Nelly's bedroom on the sixth floor and, once the door has been locked, we lie down on her bed under the poster of the actor Mathieu Kassovitz that is affixed to the wall with drawing-pins, we swallow three or four tablets of Tranxene mixed with whisky, we gaze at the coils of smoke rising slowly from our cigarettes, we imagine that we are at the seaside, in Malaga, then our eyelids fall shut and we let go, we slip our burden of weariness and boredom, and we float, we float sky-high in unreal air as if liberated from gravity, until Nelly's mother comes and bangs her fists on the door, telling us to leave the room at once or else she'll send for the fire department. Whereupon our wandering souls plummet and crash back down on the bed and are brutally awoken to the ugliness of everything. Our cigarettes have burnt holes in the bedspread.

The process-server stooped to take some books from the shelves that I had built in our bathroom library.

You have no doubt understood, Monsieur, that Mama loves books. Mama is mad about books. Mama is mad about the madness enclosed in books. Between you and me, it doesn't do her any good. Mama often says one can tell people's characters by the books they have read. People, she also says, are what they read, no need to look any further. She claims that the books one reads print themselves on our souls and alter the way we look and even change our facial features. Mama's totally nuts! She even says that the day when everybody reads great books humankind will live in peace and harmony. I'm not holding my breath!

The process-server pulled a few of the volumes from the shelf, and then, being a man of order, counted them, replaced them at once and jotted in his notebook: the Bible in two volumes; Seneca, *Letters to Lucilius*; Callimachus, *Poetry*; Epictetus, *The Handbook*; Cicero, *On Old Age*; Quintus Cicero, *Handbook for an Election Campaign*; Plutarch, *Moral Works*; Pliny the . . .

While the process-server was making his list, I thought I observed an expression of amazement on his face: his eyebrows sketched a distinctly circumflex accent of surprise. No doubt he was astounded to discover that our library contained not a single contemporary novel.

Are you disconcerted, Monsieur, by our choice of books? It's on account of Mama who will no longer read any but ancient authors. She has decreed that all literature written after 1940 is detestable. And she's quite intransigent. But what about so-and-so, I say to her, he's so inspired, so forthright? and then what about what's-her-name, she's so full of love for humankind? Detestable, Mama says, with very few exceptions. But what about this guy, who's won prizes? and that guy, whose books are bestsellers? Grocers, she says. Cowards. Their backbones are so weak, their backs are permanently bowed. Always eager to lick the boots of those they mistakenly refer to as critics, or to sell their souls for a couple of lines in a review by Rabatet, to crawl and fawn when censured by Heller, all the while posing as geniuses for some publicity blurb. My God, Mama says, such a waste of paper! forests felled for nothing!

These, Monsieur, are theories I utterly refute. And which, to be truthful, sicken me. Such a lack of discrimination, one might as well admit it, horrifies me. But, as you've seen for yourself, there's no way of changing my mother's view. Her passion overwhelms her judgement and there isn't a sensible argument that can touch her raving. Mama, you have to know, is never wrong.

I am consequently forced, Monsieur, if I am to satisfy my imaginative appetites, which are considerable, not to say unbridled, especially when it comes to sex, either to fall back on such ancient writers as Seneca, Callimachus, Pindar, or Marcel Proust, the only writers allowed past my mother's customs post, or find some cunning way to smuggle in the books that Nelly lends me and which treat the only subject which is of any real interest to me: thwarted love and its associated themes.

But I was unable to explain myself any further, for Mama came hurtling into the bathroom, beside herself with rage, her hideous fanny pack worn like a shield over her filthy nightdress, and began to yell, There's no way he's filching my books, the bastard! Anything but that! Anything but that! She was losing her temper. Yet again. Eighteen years she'd been exhausting me with her tantrums! I was sick and tired of it and was getting ready to tell her so, when the process-server opened his carp's mouth to say that he wished immediately, and finally, to visit our kitchen. He seemed determined not to let anything distract his attention.

TWENTY-TWO

At this announcement, I felt my strength ebb away. I deployed the little that remained to totter toward the kitchen and, with an engaging air (even though I was really just a ball of shame, yet more shame and mortification) I placed my hand on the doorknob. I was seized for a moment by the idea of bluntly refusing him access and, like Filo, of shouting out in Spanish *No pasarán*, but I did the precise opposite, stepping aside and murmuring in a faltering voice, Do come in, Mr Process-Server, I beg you.

The spectacle that greeted our eyes was beyond belief. A sink full of dirty plates, books lying strewn around, ashtrays overflowing with cigarette butts, egg shells, bread crusts, vegetable peelings, leftovers littering the table, soiled tea towels, a scattering of garbage, bespattered walls, just mess, dirt, filth, poverty, and destitution.

The process-server observed the foul dump without a single muscle moving in his face and, walking over to the cooker, A rabbit? he inquired, coolly indicating the animal that was shut up in the oven.

Yes Monsieur, his name is Jason, I stuttered, hiding behind my hand an ashamed smile. I do hope you won't take offense, I apologized. Mama (I laid the blame on her yet again), Mama had this absurd idea (the idea, in fact, had been mine) of turning the cooker oven, which after all wasn't being used for anything, into a rabbit hutch. All she had to do was replace the oven door with some wire netting, just as she saw Filo do in 1940, and then stick the rabbit in there, though I must emphasize, I said to make the situation appear less incongruous, that Jason is earmarked exclusively for our own domestic consumption. I was lying, obviously.

The process-server, who had no doubt seen rabbits before, coolly replied to me that a rabbit, alive moreover, could in no case be deemed an article of furniture and accordingly need make no appearance in the present inventory.

I breathed a sigh of relief.

At that precise moment I heard my mother, who for several minutes now had been patrolling the living room, explode in a torrent of atrocious abuse. The process-server and I strained our ears to hear, while our gaze fell idiotically on the wall separating the kitchen from the living room. My mother was probably arguing with one of the ghosts that haunted her memory. I was used to such fights. The reproaches and invective that she was hurling at her invisible assailant seemed to include, as best I could hear, the words looter and thief as well as several filthier terms which my sense of decorum prevents me from transcribing here.

It won't have escaped you, I said to the process-server, that my mother's condition has scarcely improved over time. In the days following the death of Bousquet, who was assassinated on June 8, 1993, by a certain Christian Didier, I believed, stupidly, that my mother's madness would now relent. And that life, real life, would return.

I was mistaken.

My mother's condition only got worse. For she now found herself deprived of the purpose that she had passionately served day in day out throughout these fifteen years. This historical project, as she termed it, this project that had so swallowed her up that she became lost and was consumed, this project, however extravagant it had been, had granted her a footing, a purpose, a fulcrum in the midst of nothingness. The pursuit of all those whom, in her avenging rage, she called monsters had constituted her law, her intemperance and the justification for her life. To find herself thus deprived left her disoriented, vacillating and, as it were, dislodged from her destiny. And her craziness, deprived now of any outlet, rather than drying up, as was hoped, blazed out of control.

Mama became ever more entangled in her ravings, professing that if the death of Putain had made no difference to this world it was because, at his back, there lurked something larger, something unimaginable and diabolical, a malign and infinite force of which nobody knew the cause, an unbridled and ungovernable power, a tidal wave, a fury that respected neither God, home nor master and which she absolutely had to discover. Pure madness.

But to escape from this vision which, deep down, filled her with dismay, my mother plunged deeper into the mire of a past whose horror possessed at least the advantage of familiarity. She clung to it as though it were the only solid ground. And there she found a constant haven from the unforeseen events of the present and the terrifying threats of the future.

War was now her dwelling place, the world her enemy. She was one, they were a thousand. You had to open your eyes. And know what you were looking for.

From that point on she refused to leave the apartment, endlessly checking all doors and windows with the utmost circumspection, listening out for the sound of boots or the whining of stukas overhead, conversing with the dead, wandering among the ghosts and addressing screaming indictments at the television whenever she thought she had caught a glimpse of Putain, whom the latest TV techniques, she asserted, rendered unrecognizable to any but the most practiced eye.

But in spite of it all she did not become resigned. She had a confused and in some sense instinctive premonition that to lay down arms in the face of evil would be to accept death. And my mother could never reconcile herself to dying. Not tomorrow, not ever. Of all the different forms that her madness assumed, this was the only one that gave me any comfort. My mother never grew weary of the sensation of being alive. Because her soul, I believe, was both old and very young.

And her war against evil became her war against death.

My mother persevered in her insane struggle but without having the faintest idea how to go about it, given that a madman, she fulminated, had assassinated Putain in her place. She still wanted to redeem the world and restore its innocence. But how can you redeem the world, she said to herself, when you are the only one who wants it to be redeemed and the only weapon you have is a lousy little pistol?

Mama found herself confronted with concerns that were so elevated, floating at such unbelievable altitudes, that she finally lost all grip on reality. Day-to-day troubles no longer had any hold on her. So who had to deal with them? Yours truly, I said, pressing an angry finger against my chest while the process-server, simultaneously pulling in both his stomach and his backside, attempted to slip through to the refrigerator.

He jotted down its brand name: Siemens, its height: 1.20 m., its width: 50 cm. But just as he was preparing to examine its contents, Mama materialized at the door, a cigarette butt between her lips.

Infuriated, she declared that any inventory of the products
contained in the refrigerator would necessarily be very rapid
for the very good reason, she shouted, that the said refrigerator was utterly empty. Do you think it amuses me to see my
Louisiane reduced to this wartime diet? she shouted at the
process-server's back. Do you think my maternal heart doesn't
bleed? I too should like to shower my daughter with gifts. I
too should like from time to time to buy her a chocolate Pop-
sicle, a meal at a Chinese restaurant, shoes with platform heels
like the ones her friend Nelly wears, different fancy clothes for
each day of the week, a TV with fifty-nine channels so she can
wallow in the romantic soaps she so adores, not to mention a
motorized land vehicle, she said with a sad laugh, so she can
go and enjoy herself on the Côte d'Azur.

My mother fell silent for a moment. I thought her anger had
abated. Then, as if a fresh wave of rage was rising to her lips,
she commanded the process-server to inscribe on his bullshit
inventory, quote, that we live on a grand total of, write it down!
3,000 cachectic francs a month that the National Rescue Plan
pays us and which we spend as follows, write it down! she
yelled at the back of the process-server, who recoiled invol-
untarily: first, a sum of approximately 400 francs per week
on basic foodstuffs: bread, rice, pasta, potatoes, eggs, minced
beef, sugar, chocolate, and Coca-Cola; second, I forgot the
Nescafé, second, a sum earmarked for our cigarettes ration,
a sum of how much? all you have to do is count! Her growing fury was reddening her cheeks. A pack of Gauloises for
me, plus a pack of Marlboros for my daughter who smokes in
secret, that makes two packs a day which multiplied by seven
makes fourteen packets a week which multiplied by 20 francs
makes 280 francs, 280 francs plus 400 francs multiplied by

four makes how many? makes 2,720 francs out of the 3,000 francs that the National Rescue Plan gives us, you see what's left! she shouted bringing her face up perilously close to the process-server's back. Never mind how careful we are to use our cigarette ends to make new cigarettes and to eat rice one day and potatoes the next, we're broke!

What recourse do I have? she screamed, seizing the vegetable peeler and pressing it against the process-server's occiput. The process-server was transformed into a statue of salt. A letter to Putain, like the one Filo sent, she yelled, begging them to send me a food parcel?

Mama, I entreated.

Madame, the process-server said.

TWENTY-THREE

There is no Madame here, my mother exploded, what there is is a madwoman who is about to beat your brains out.

And grabbing the process-server brutally by one shoulder, she spun him round, slapped him in the face, pinned him against the refrigerator, threw his spectacles to the ground and stamped on them, there! It happened very quickly. Help me, my mother said and, as if the suppressed rage, fear, and torments of an entire lifetime had coalesced to form an immeasurable, savage, and devastating force, she clasped him by his lapels, hoisted him off the floor, and dragged him from the room, as though he were some ordinary parcel.

And I who, since the very start of these proceedings, had taken the utmost care not to strike any attitude that could be interpreted as insolence or impropriety, I who had striven to mollify this monster with a thousand polite attentions in the hope of inducing him to show some compassion, I don't know what came over me, I hurled myself upon him, without a moment's hesitation, without stopping to think, I gripped him by his jacket and pushed with all my strength against his back while Mama yanked him forward by his tie.

We forced him through the living room, zigzagging between the furniture and the potted plants. We roared with laughter to see him staggering and thrashing about. We called a brief halt to catch our breath, securing him with an iron hand. Mama, he looks like he wants to talk. He'd better not try, my mother said, a wicked person who remains silent is like a toothless wolf, now who said that, my dear? Suetonius, I told her. We resumed our slalom run, laughing ever more merrily. We propelled him down the narrow corridor with an energy I hadn't known we possessed, but joy and anger, I learned in that instant, multiply our strength many times over. Before opening the door, my mother, quoting Marcus Cato, sagely declared, One should act toward an evil person, as a sailor toward a whirlwind. And with these fine words, we cast him out. Into the whirlwind.

SOME USEFUL ADVICE FOR APPRENTICE PROCESS-SERVERS

Some people think that our work is malicious and that we are the poor's most implacable enemies. But no critics will ever succeed in challenging what we know to be true. Besides, we believe that all such attacks are designed to undermine Justice. For we *are* Justice, and whoever attacks us, attacks Justice. Even if much worse things were said about us, we would still continue to practice our profession with dedication and enthusiasm.

Don't listen to such remarks but instead devote yourselves to your work which is to serve the Law and to be its arm. Its secular arm.

Be courageous because the work is hard.

And don't lie to yourselves. The advantages envious people attribute to our profession are derisory when compared to its disadvantages. It's my duty to warn you: the situations that you will face will be worse than your worst nightmares.

Whenever possible, begin your job early in the morning.

Having gone into a dirty building, you will ride an elevator that's been vandalized and walk down corridors whose walls are covered with graffiti depicting genitalia in horribly realistic detail.

You will be afraid.

But hide your fear.

Having found the door, clearly announce your arrival. Be calm. Knock and say: Maître Echinard or Maître Whoever, process-server-at-law. There's no need for eloquence.

To be effective, you must take them completely by surprise. After an initial period of astonishment, lasting normally between two and ten minutes, you may hear the sound of people stampeding in all directions, muffled cries, scuttling movements, furniture being shifted, a panic that in the eyes of honest people confirms the guilt of those inside. Remain calm. Take your time. Have the patience of a hunter. Lie in wait.

Once the door is open, be doubly careful. Process-servers have been knocked over the head and thrown down the stairs before they had a chance to read their official orders.

Read out loud your *Order to Evacuate*, in a most neutral tone. Be careful not to irritate the people. Those about to be evicted are, it seems, much more touchy than the average person. State clearly: I, Maître Echinard, process-server-at-law, hereby order Monsieur Marcel Turpin, or whatever his name is, immediately and without delay to evacuate the premises of all goods and occupants, so that the claimant may dispose of them as he deems fit, etcetera, etcetera.

Do not be surprised if this order, despite its clarity, is not understood by these people who, in most cases, are illiterate. But with the astounding intuition that the poor (similar in this regard to animals) bring to detecting threats and harassment, they will immediately realize that they have no recourse and must leave as soon as possible.

It is at this point that the usual wailing and gnashing of teeth begins, the endless whining, the tearful pleading, the children torn from their cradles to make you feel sorry for them, in short, a vulgar exhibition of the most repugnant misery. Don't allow yourselves to be moved by this display of misery. Let them howl. But don't rush things. If their emotional outburst strikes you as lasting too long—the poor, as you will realize, are often overemotional, which helps to account for their poor social success—if their emotion is prolonged, I was saying, tell them in a firm voice that should it prove necessary the police will be called upon to intervene. That'll soon calm them down.

I'm duty-bound to warn you that you'll be exposed, especially during domestic evictions, to every kind of petty, nasty harassment. Such is our lot in life.

To give you just one concrete example, last month I had to enforce a seizure order at the home of an individual well known to our department who, arguing that he was still head of his household, absolutely refused to switch on the light. This deplorable lack of good manners forced me to work in almost total darkness, bumping into furniture whose period and style I was unable to identify correctly. I was forced, further, after examining each object, to go out into the building's ill-lit hallway in order to take the notes for my report. I made (I was counting them) twenty-six trips back and forth between the apartment and the hallway! I left the place completely exhausted.

The very same day, another tenant, using the same reasoning, hammered away on saucepan lids for the entire two hours that it took me to complete my work. He said, sarcastically, that, first of all, he was within his rights—and I had to concede that indeed he was—and that, in the second place, he just loved percussion, which, he stated, hadn't as yet been prohibited by any law. There was nothing I could do about this, and so by the time I left his apartment my brain felt like mush.

Last Thursday, an old woman, at whose home I had arrived to execute a distraining order with a view to an auction, began shouting obscenities, pretending she was scolding her cat. I knew perfectly well that the obscenities were directed at me.

I must emphasize to you that you have the power to file an official complaint against any tenant who insults *you*. But on one condition: the insult has to be addressed specifically at you. Addressing it to a cat, to a wall, or to any other third party is a ruse against which you have no recourse in law.

Speaking of cats and other domestic animals (of which, I should say, the lowly and the needy are exceedingly fond), remember that, like children, they have immunity from distraining orders. French law, in its clemency, even goes so far as to prohibit the confiscation of any articles of furniture upon which bird cages, aquaria, or other miscellaneous pet boxes have been placed. Regardless of what we may think of this law, we have no choice but to comply with it, especially in view of the fact that its provisions are familiar to almost every individual with whom we have to deal.

To our utter astonishment, note that tenants, even though they are completely uneducated, in fact appear to be perfectly versed in regulations that are to their advantage. And they shamelessly exploit them. The proof of it is: their homes are always overrun with animals! The apartments that we visit are infested with cats, dogs, chickens, ducks, rabbits, sheep, mynah birds, parrots, and countless little babies, all squealing, meowing, and bleating like it's some kind of competition. It's typical to find bathrooms turned into hen houses, and bedrooms into stables. Do you suppose that the people there complain about having such neighbors? Never! I've even come across immigrant families who, for purely commercial reasons, were keeping veritable menageries within their four walls. I'll let you imagine for yourselves the filth in which they wallowed!

I will repeat this, since it's very important: most tenants know the laws that favor them and, however ignorant they may be otherwise, are able to cite them with no difficulty. And not only do they know the laws that favor them, but they are also able, with incredible skill, to twist those laws that were created to be used against them. Mark my words: there are even some people who are experts at such distortions. And we know who they are. Usually, they are intellectuals whose minds have been corrupted by prolonged idleness. Which laws do they distort to their advantage, and how? I shall confine myself to two examples.

Here's the first. All of you are acquainted with Article 184 of the Penal Code, which prohibits any use of violence against us, whether verbal or physical. Well, there are some deranged people who will go to any lengths to flout this law by inventing insidious techniques, the brutality of which cannot be clearly denounced yet that constitute a very considerable nuisance nonetheless. A Parisian writer, who shall remain nameless and whose home I was visiting for the hundredth time, kept flashing his camera at me the entire morning, and there was nothing I could do to stop him. Since this unique form of assault is not covered by any existing legal provision, I had no option but to put up with this highly unwelcome attack.

What's more, when I asked the said writer to hand me his camera so that I could make a note of its brand, he showed unbelievable insolence by calmly objecting that the camera in question was an essential tool of his trade.

French law, always inclined toward indulging people, does in fact stipulate that all goods necessary to the work of the distrainee and of his or her family, subject to the restrictions set out in article 2092, Paragraph 4, are exempt from seizure. The way in which distrainees interpret this law gives rise, as you can imagine, to some thoroughly insane situations. It's common to hear a housewife pleading "historical research" in order to hang on to a broken-down table that she pompously refers to as her desk, or saying she's doing a sociological analysis of the contemporary world in order to prevent us from taking her television. Don't be fooled by such pitiful arguments. Demand that they produce formal proof of their work. Then you'll see how quickly and pathetically their pretenses collapse.

The second example is as follows. Article L613 of the Penal Code states that the execution of eviction orders must be suspended between December first and March fifteenth every year on account of the cold weather. As if we were in Siberia! Be that as it may. In fact, this supposedly humanitarian law is subject to systematic abuse and really only serves to encourage unscrupulous tenants to commit fraud and foment trouble. Such people, always searching for new outlets for their dishonesty, proceed to default on their rents because, after all, the law practically encourages them to do so. If one's stated objective were to increase the number of offenses, one would hardly go about it any differently. And the upshot? How many poor people pay their rents during the winter? A handful! All the others save themselves the trouble. They're not idiots. But I guarantee you this! These thieves can make us wait but they can't elude their just desserts forever. For on March sixteenth, we process-servers go back on the offensive.

In psychological terms, I mean.

Because remember this: the success of an eviction depends upon the psychological skill that the process-server is able to use and on our knowledge of the tricks and cunning of which the human heart is capable.

So be psychological!

Learn how to sniff out liars, fraudsters, twisted minds, and charlatans.

Don't fall into the snare laid for you by hysterical people who throw fainting fits the moment they see you. All they want is to make you feel guilty! Don't fall for it. Tell yourselves that these supposed victims have got what they deserved.

Don't be duped by the whining of psychopaths. Genuine pain is never expressed in loud cries.

Don't yield to the blackmail of apparent misfortune. Public sorrow is phony sorrow.

Learn how to tell a true crazy from an impostor who is just trying to shock you.

For this purpose, I can't urge you too strongly to immerse yourselves, as I constantly do, in works of psychology. Without flattering myself, I should say that thanks to this study I have attained a degree of sophistication in my approach to human beings that enables me to escape unscathed from the most dangerous situations. And God knows there's no shortage of dangerous situations!

Only yesterday, I was forced to foil the plans of a certain Rose Mélie and her daughter Louisiane, two women whom I have no hesitation in describing as hellish. Acting jointly, they had contrived a plan as clever as it was twisted with the sole intention of hampering my work. And I have to admit that, were it not for the knowledge that I have acquired over the years regarding the clockwork mechanisms of the human psyche, I would immediately have fallen into their trap.

Here are the facts.

On the fifteenth of this month, I went to the Cité des Acacias housing project where most of our clients are concentrated.

Filthy building, grimy hallways, nauseating elevator. A routine job.

I knocked. I stated my name. The door opened. So far, nothing out of the ordinary. But as soon as I had begun my inventory, an old alcoholic, faking madness, accused me of being a militiaman acting on the orders of Darnand. Do you know who Darnand was? Is there *anybody* here who knows who Darnand was? I don't see any hands. Darnand, Ladies and Gentleman, was the Head of the Militia in 1942 and then the General Secretary for the Maintenance of Order from 1943 to 1944. You can see at once the vile and willful confusion that this old woman was seeking to create in an attempt to humiliate me, demean me, and arouse in me remorse or guilt. That was her intention. I need hardly tell you that to me these insinuations were like water off a duck's back. But I was forced for two whole hours to put up with the flood of her perfidious allusions, all of which sought to establish a parallel between my professional activities and the much-disparaged actions of the Militia. Shielding herself from any judicial proceedings by pretending to be insane, she felt free to spew out an uninterrupted stream of the most appalling insults. And not only did she go on about such controversial characters as Darnand, whom she maliciously associated with me, but also a number of great figures from our nation's history, including Marshal Pétain himself, whom she, in her vulgarity, nicknamed, forgive me, "Marshal Putain." This slut, for I have omitted to say that the aforesaid Rose was sickeningly dirty, this slut, I was saying, on broaching the subject of the Collaboration, turned into one of the Furies, screaming, gesticulating, and shouting at me brutally.

And, for what seemed like an eternity, I had to listen to her heap the most terrible insults on the man who governed our country with dignity from 1940 to 1944. And I had to witness her trample all over the ideals that make our nation so wonderful. And I had to listen (without replying) as she ridiculed true values and dragged the virtues of self-denial and sacrifice through the mire. Her intention, as I quickly realized, was to shock me, disorient me, while attacking the principles on which any process-server bases his life, his work, and his morality. She hoped to make it impossible for me to complete my inventory correctly. A Machiavellian ploy! But I wasn't fooled for long!

Further, she implied, that, given the high salary we're paid, process-servers in effect steal with impunity, and that the authority we have to enter other people's homes amounts to nothing less than rape! A thief and a rapist! I was laughing inside at such accusations, but I didn't let anything show.

To complicate matters even more, while the mother tried to wrongfoot me psychologically, her daughter Louisiane tried to seduce me by her provocative behavior: lascivious glances, sexual allusions, wiggling her rear-end, and lustful stares. This little slut, similar in looks to many you run into in our housing projects, with her red hair, black nails and sexy little skirt, was hoping to excite me and make me fall for her charms, and so forget the job I had come to do.

You won't be surprised when I tell you that this young woman was disappointed. As was her mother. Faced with these psychological and sexual attacks, the sort of thing that would have worked on most men, I was as impassive as a statue and responded to their provocations with silence. In the end they caved in.

But I'd be misleading you if I let you imagine that the pathological conditions we encounter during the course of our work are always fake. From time to time we do come across the real thing, I mean a complete nut whose dangerousness has been confirmed by doctors.

Faced with individuals of this type, you are advised to use, if I may put it like this, your finest set of tweezers.

Take special care with depressed people. Be wary of their potential for bizarre behavior: they may have an anxiety attack, jump out the window, chew up and then swallow the distraining order, don't laugh, I've seen such things on more than one occasion, they may hang themselves, stick their heads in a gas oven, or attempt suicide in some other way.

Depressed people and their suicide attempts are the bane of every process-server's life and a constant worry. If a depressed person decides, for example, to throw himself out the window right there in front of you, that creates a real mess for you! Which is precisely what they're trying to do, in their bitter, twisted way: to turn the situation on its head and make *you* the villain. Whether or not they really intend to kill themselves is a moot point.

In such circumstances, stay calm and collected. Talk in a reassuring but firm manner. And refer the person at once to both a psychiatrist and a social worker, two such precautions being better than one.

Take another case: someone with paranoia.

What is a paranoid person? Do you know what paranoia is? Nobody knows what paranoia is?

A paranoid, take notes on this, is an individual, usually Spanish, who refuses to open the door to you. Or who opens it with a sawed-off shotgun aimed at your chest.

Confronted with lunatics like this, there's only one response: call the police! And without delay!

Are you anxiously wondering if there are many such nuts running around? I'll give you a straight answer: no, there aren't! Most of the people who are served with *Orders to Evacuate* turn out, upon getting to know them, to be inoffensive and all the turmoil they make is really just a way of dealing with their anxiety.

Whatever the circumstances, remain calm and use diplomacy. The law requires you to act "as good family-men and fathers," that's the exact phrase. What does it mean? That whatever happens, you must remain calm and diplomatic.

Calm and diplomatic, these are the watchwords of our profession. I'll add a third, which you are all expecting: fair. Do not discriminate in any way among those you evict. Whether young or old, black or white, fit or disabled, enforce the law fairly.

And refrain from any commentary! You'll be tempted to give these people advice, excuse their vulgarity, or rub their faces in their own filth. Because, let's not kid ourselves, the vast majority of those evicted have deserved, what am I saying, have worked at, have striven, have struggled to achieve this condition, indulging year in year out in a life of disorder, anarchy, and laziness, both physical and moral. All you have to do is go into their home to realize this fact. Dirt, disorder, decay, and terrible smells are typical. In the case of Rose Mélie and her daughter's apartment, which I was mentioning to you just now, the only term to describe it is *devastation*. Devastation pure and simple.

At least if these poor people showed some disdain for worldly goods! If they showed off their lack of interest, as they should do! But no! Losing two rickety chairs has them weeping buckets and when they see their beloved TV being carted off, their despair is boundless. It's pathetic.

But our duty, this needs to be stated over and over again, is not at all to judge them or to express personal feelings. It is our job, in a sense, to disappear behind the cover of the Law, as far as that is possible. I am tired of having to keep making such obvious points.

Sometimes a process-server's knock on the door may get no response. You then have no choice but to shout loudly from your side of the door that, in accordance with Article 587 of the New Code of Procedure, the door may be opened, if need be, with the assistance of a locksmith accompanied by a police officer. This announcement has a miraculous effect. Personally, however, it's rare for me to resort to such a tactic. I can't encourage you strongly enough, Ladies and Gentlemen, to follow my example in this regard. First and foremost, seek to negotiate. Try human contact. You will be rewarded.

Only rarely, as I was saying, do I have to use extreme measures. The fact is that, contrary to public belief, it's unusual for those facing eviction to rebel. In ninety-nine-point-nine percent of cases, the person being evicted complies with the order without offering the least resistance. Imagine for one second the danger that would face our nation if all those evicted suddenly decided to resist eviction and to form a common front. Guaranteed chaos.

But don't worry, Ladies and Gentlemen, about any such thing. Poor people obey orders. It's a fact. They may grumble a bit, sure, but they obey. Knock on wood. There remain those extremely rare cases of fanatic rebels who remain legendary within our profession and provide it with its hours of glory. I shall speak to you of these little rebellions and the means for quelling them in a future lesson. For now, all I need tell you is that these little rebellions always end very badly indeed for those who lead them. As you might well imagine.

But I should like to conclude today's lesson on a comforting note: so-called straightforward evictions.

So-called straightforward evictions involve, for the most part, elderly persons. We process-servers would all concur with the view that evictions of elderly persons are certainly the quickest and the easiest. Every day we observe that elderly persons in fact receive their eviction orders with a profound sense of acceptance as though, deep down, they were overjoyed at the idea of escaping their awful little boxes and of being lodged in homes where meals and heating are provided round the clock. Believe me, it is good work that we do. I would like you to keep that in mind.

And to finish, a little bit of fun. We shall now consider the matter of adultery reports. I can see your faces brightening up already.

Alas, it is with increasing infrequency that our services are called upon to provide adultery reports. Adultery reports are threatened with extinction. As morals become looser, so adultery reports become rarer. We process-servers vigorously deplore this increasing rarity. For adultery reports could always be relied upon to add some spice to the life of the process-server, who more often than not is confronted with situations devoid of anything remotely amusing. Adultery reports were always a source of comical, indeed thrilling, situations, bringing a little merriment into an occupation that, it has to be acknowledged, is seldom merry. Until quite recently, process-servers could always recall some funny anecdote relating to an adultery report and thus, when invited to a dinner party, were able to entertain their fellow guests.

But let us not mourn our past. Let us celebrate instead our present times, since circumstances requiring our assistance increase from day to day. In our town alone, we have recorded seventy-two eviction orders this year versus sixty-one last year! An increase of eleven! What other business is doing this well right now? I don't know of one.

And if the joys of yesteryear are gone for good, your chosen profession will afford you satisfactions of quite another kind. That of knowing, Ladies and Gentlemen, that you are making an active contribution to Public Order, without which society can't survive. Above all that of knowing that while humankind is not exempt from vice, weakness, and stupidity, it has at least equipped itself with the means, thanks to us, thanks to you, of limiting their disastrous effects.

It is with these optimistic words that I shall conclude my lecture, which, as you will have realized for yourselves, has been no mere recitation of recommended working methods, but a veritable philosophy lesson.

See you all next week.

Lydie Salvayre, the daughter of refugees from the Spanish Civil War, grew up in the south of France where she attended medical school and received a degree in psychiatry. It wasn't until she was in her mid-forties that she published her first novel, *The Declaration*. Since that time she has published nine other books, including *Everyday Life*, *The Lecture*, and *The Power of Flies*. She has received numerous accolades and awards in France for her fiction, including the Prix Hermes for *The Declaration*, and the Prix Novembre for *The Company of Ghosts*.

FOR A FULL LIST OF PUBLICATIONS, VISIT:
www.dalkeyarchive.com

CAROLE MASO, *AVA*.

LADISLAV MATEJKA AND KRYSTYNA POMORSKA, EDS.,
Readings in Russian Poetics: Formalist and Structuralist Views.

HARRY MATHEWS,
The Case of the Persevering Maltese: Collected Essays.
Cigarettes.
The Conversions.
The Human Country: New and Collected Stories.
The Journalist.
My Life in CIA.
Singular Pleasures.
The Sinking of the Odradek Stadium.
Tlooth.
20 Lines a Day.

ROBERT L. MCLAUGHLIN, ED.,
Innovations: An Anthology of Modern & Contemporary Fiction.

STEVEN MILLHAUSER, *The Barnum Museum*.
In the Penny Arcade.

RALPH J. MILLS, JR., *Essays on Poetry*.

OLIVE MOORE, *Spleen*.

NICHOLAS MOSLEY, *Accident*.
Assassins.
Catastrophe Practice.
Children of Darkness and Light.
The Hesperides Tree.
Hopeful Monsters.
Imago Bird.
Impossible Object.
Inventing God.
Judith.
Look at the Dark.
Natalie Natalia.
Serpent.
The Uses of Slime Mould: Essays of Four Decades.

WARREN F. MOTTE, JR.,
Fables of the Novel: French Fiction since 1990.
Oulipo: A Primer of Potential Literature.

YVES NAVARRE, *Our Share of Time*.

DOROTHY NELSON, *Tar and Feathers*.

WILFRIDO D. NOLLEDO, *But for the Lovers*.

FLANN O'BRIEN, *At Swim-Two-Birds*.
At War.
The Best of Myles.
The Dalkey Archive.
Further Cuttings.
The Hard Life.
The Poor Mouth.
The Third Policeman.

CLAUDE OLLIER, *The Mise-en-Scène*.

PATRIK OUŘEDNÍK, *Europeana*.

FERNANDO DEL PASO, *Palinuro of Mexico*.

ROBERT PINGET, *The Inquisitory*.
Mahu or The Material.
Trio.

RAYMOND QUENEAU, *The Last Days*.
Odile.
Pierrot Mon Ami.
Saint Glinglin.

ANN QUIN, *Berg*.
Passages.
Three.
Tripticks.

ISHMAEL REED, *The Free-Lance Pallbearers*.
The Last Days of Louisiana Red.
Reckless Eyeballing.
The Terrible Threes.
The Terrible Twos.
Yellow Back Radio Broke-Down.

JULIÁN RÍOS, *Larva: A Midsummer Night's Babel*.
Poundemonium.

AUGUSTO ROA BASTOS, *I the Supreme*.

JACQUES ROUBAUD, *The Great Fire of London*.

Hortense in Exile.
Hortense Is Abducted.
The Plurality of Worlds of Lewis.
The Princess Hoppy.
Some Thing Black.

LEON S. ROUDIEZ, *French Fiction Revisited*.

VEDRANA RUDAN, *Night*.

LYDIE SALVAYRE, *The Company of Ghosts*.
The Lecture.

LUIS RAFAEL SÁNCHEZ, *Macho Camacho's Beat*.

SEVERO SARDUY, *Cobra & Maitreya*.

NATHALIE SARRAUTE, *Do You Hear Them?*
Martereau.
The Planetarium.

ARNO SCHMIDT, *Collected Stories*.
Nobodaddy's Children.

CHRISTINE SCHUTT, *Nightwork*.

GAIL SCOTT, *My Paris*.

JUNE AKERS SEESE,
Is This What Other Women Feel Too?
What Waiting Really Means.

AURELIE SHEEHAN, *Jack Kerouac Is Pregnant*.

VIKTOR SHKLOVSKY, *Knight's Move*.
A Sentimental Journey: Memoirs 1917-1922.
Theory of Prose.
Third Factory.
Zoo, or Letters Not about Love.

JOSEF ŠKVORECKÝ,
The Engineer of Human Souls.

CLAUDE SIMON, *The Invitation*.

GILBERT SORRENTINO, *Aberration of Starlight*.
Blue Pastoral.
Crystal Vision.
Imaginative Qualities of Actual Things.
Mulligan Stew.
Pack of Lies.
The Sky Changes.
Something Said.
Splendide-Hôtel.
Steelwork.
Under the Shadow.

W. M. SPACKMAN, *The Complete Fiction*.

GERTRUDE STEIN, *Lucy Church Amiably*.
The Making of Americans.
A Novel of Thank You.

PIOTR SZEWC, *Annihilation*.

STEFAN THEMERSON, *Hobson's Island*.
Tom Harris.

JEAN-PHILIPPE TOUSSAINT, *Television*.

ESTHER TUSQUETS, *Stranded*.

DUBRAVKA UGRESIC, *Lend Me Your Character*.
Thank You for Not Reading.

MATI UNT, *Things in the Night*.

LUISA VALENZUELA, *He Who Searches*.

BORIS VIAN, *Heartsnatcher*.

PAUL WEST, *Words for a Deaf Daughter & Gala*.

CURTIS WHITE, *America's Magic Mountain*.
The Idea of Home.
Memories of My Father Watching TV.
Monstrous Possibility: An Invitation to Literary Politics.
Requiem.

DIANE WILLIAMS, *Excitability: Selected Stories*.
Romancer Erector.

DOUGLAS WOOLF, *Wall to Wall*.
Ya! & John-Juan.

PHILIP WYLIE, *Generation of Vipers*.

MARGUERITE YOUNG, *Angel in the Forest*.
Miss MacIntosh, My Darling.

REYOUNG, *Unbabbling*.

ZORAN ŽIVKOVIĆ, *Hidden Camera*.

LOUIS ZUKOFSKY, *Collected Fiction*.

SCOTT ZWIREN, *God Head*.